W9-BKO-694

THE HAUNTING OF GREY HILLS
Sinews of thy Heart

JENNIFER SKOGEN

EPIC
Press

Sinews of Thy Heart
The Haunting of Grey Hills: Book #4

Written by Jennifer Skogen

Copyright © 2016 by Abdo Consulting Group, Inc.

Published by EPIC Press™
PO Box 398166
Minneapolis, MN 55439

Cover design by Dorothy Toth
Images for cover art obtained from iStockPhoto.com
Edited by Melanie Austin

LIBRARY OF CONGRESS CATALOGING-IN-PUBLICATION DATA

Skogen, Jennifer.
Sinews of thy heart / Jennifer Skogen.
p. cm. — (The haunting of Grey Hills ; #4)
Summary: After the tragedy on Halloween, Jackson must decide if he should stay in
Grey Hills, or pack up everything and leave with Sam and the others. When Jackson
starts sleepwalking and hearing voices, he isn't sure if he is going crazy, or if he has
inherited an unspeakable power while, Claire is determined to find out exactly what
happened on Halloween.
ISBN 978-1-68076-032-3 (hardcover)
1. Ghosts—Fiction. 2. High schools—Fiction. 3. Supernatural—Fiction.
4. Haunted places—Fiction. 5. Young adult fiction. I. Title.
[Fic]—dc23
2015932722

EPICPRESS.COM

To the best friends a girl could ask for

Prologue

1916

Eli Grey sat at his kitchen table and pressed the tip of a carving knife into the soft skin beneath his right forearm. It wasn't a deep cut—just enough so a sheen of red coated the edge of the knife. It didn't even hurt, not with his blood simmering in his veins, and the growing light of dawn tugging at his skin. Eli was on the edge of the precipice now. Nothing in this world could hurt him.

Holding the knife above his open journal, Eli let his blood drip into the spine. Three large drops, right in the center of the book. Next, Eli plucked three hairs from his head and pressed them between the pages where his sticky, drying blood would hold them fast. Bone fragments from a shattered toe had already been ground up and mixed in with the ink.

Now, finally, it was complete.

He didn't feel any different, holding his Token in his own hands. Eli wasn't sure what, exactly, he expected. That the pages would vibrate or throb in time with his heart? That he would feel a part of his soul caught in the pages of his journal?

That was the point, wasn't it? Eli's body was going to die, but his spirit would be bound to this world. That was the only option left.

Taking up his pen, Eli began to write his final entry, which was actually a letter:

Dearest Mabel,

He paused. All the words he had planned now felt utterly inadequate. How could he explain what he had to do? The cut on his arm must have been deeper than he thought because a thin line of blood ran down to his wrist and pooled onto the worn wood of the table. He would have to clean it up before he left.

Finally Eli wrote:

Dearest Mabel,
Death is not the end.
I am still here.

Chapter One

Jackson didn't know where they buried Macy's body.

He asked Sam, the morning after Halloween. Day of the fucking Dead. He begged her, actually.

It was five in the morning and they were drinking, just him and Sam—tossing back shots like they were water instead of whiskey. Water of Life. That's what they called whiskey. Jackson had read that somewhere. Dom refused to come out of his room, and Trev was already passed out on the couch.

"Where is she?" Jackson asked, knowing he

was very drunk, but not feeling it exactly. His words were coming out of his mouth too slowly. "Please." His throat tightened, and he wiped tears off his face. Jackson hadn't realized he was crying. "What'd you do with her?"

Sam's eyes were red. None of them had slept. "I can't tell you."

"Why?" He tried to pick up the empty shot glass but it spun away from his fingers. "Where is she?" he asked again.

"Jackson. I can't keep telling you this." She took his hand in both of hers and held it there, pressed down on the table. He couldn't really feel his fingers, but he could tell her hands were cold. "You were covered in her blood. Your fingerprints are all over her. They're going to think you killed her."

"But I didn't."

When they found Jackson, he was still holding Macy. Dom had tried to pull her body away from him, screaming at him, but Jackson wouldn't let go.

What did you do? That's what Dom had kept screaming. *What did you do to her?*

"I know," Sam said. Something green clung to the collar of Sam's shirt. A piece of cedar tree? Did they bury her in the woods? "But they can't ever find her. They can't even know she's dead. They'll blame you."

Jackson sat for a long time, staring at Sam's hands wrapped around his own. There was school soon, but he couldn't go to school because Macy was dead. Her parents probably thought she'd stayed over at Claire's, and Claire probably thought Macy had stayed over with Dom, so no one knew yet.

Jesus, her parents.

"I need to tell her parents. They need to know." Jackson pulled his hand away and pressed the tips of his fingers to his eye sockets. He was getting a headache—the kind that felt like it was pressing out from behind his eyes.

Sam shook her head. Again. "You can't, Jackson. You aren't supposed to know anything about this. You get that, right? You weren't there. You don't know where Macy is. She must have run away."

Macy would never have run away from anything. Jackson wanted to tell Sam that, but even with all the whiskey, he knew that wasn't the point. And his head . . . it just kept pounding and pounding, like something was knocking on the inside of his brain.

Jackson closed his eyes and saw the Door closing. The light from the Door had been so bright. Excruciatingly bright. He thought he was going to be lost in it. But then he had felt someone touch his face, right before the Door closed.

That was really when his headache had started, he realized. When the Door slammed shut in his face. Someone had touched him, coming between him and the terrible light of the Door. Was it . . . could it have been Macy?

"But where is she?" he asked again, and Sam's eyes filled with tears. She didn't answer him this time. Instead, she got up and climbed into his lap.

She was heavy, but it was a nice kind of weight—like he knew he was still there, in his body, and not floating away to wherever his pounding head was trying to send him. Sam wrapped her arms around his neck and pressed her face into his shoulder. She sobbed, and he held her, smoothing her long hair down her back.

"It's okay." he whispered, but he wasn't talking to Sam. He was back in the woods, as Macy's life drained through his fingers. "You're okay."

As he held Sam, for an instant he thought he saw something above his head. A soft, blue light. But when he looked up all he saw was the unbroken white of the ceiling. He blinked a few times, but couldn't quite shake the feeling that there was something there, right above him. Something he couldn't quite see.

◦◦◦◦

Jackson went home before going to school. He was still drunk and so tired that his hands shook as he unlocked the front door. The TV was on in the living room, but he didn't see his dad anywhere. He must have already left for work and forgot to turn off the news. Did his dad even know that Jackson never came home last night?

The air smelled like coffee, and for a moment, Jackson thought he was going to be sick right there in the entryway. Jackson pressed the back of his hand over his mouth until the wave of nausea passed.

He had an hour before class started, and he needed to take a shower and change his clothes. Trev's clothes, actually. Sam made Jackson put all his old clothes into a bag, even his shoes, and gave him some of her brother's clothes to wear home. The jeans were way too short on him, and a little loose in the waist. It looked like he'd had a sudden growth spurt.

Glancing down at his bare ankles, Jackson wanted to tell Macy how ridiculous he looked. She was always teasing him about how tall he was, and especially how skinny he was. Macy would have made him stand there while she took his picture.

In the bathroom, Jackson took off Trev's clothes and looked at himself in the mirror. What he saw would have scared him, if he didn't already feel so numb. Jackson's face was greenish, and when he looked at his hands, he noticed a speck of blood in the webbing between his finger and thumb.

Jackson picked at the spec of blood until his skin was raw. He took a deep breath and held it until it felt like his lungs might burst. Then he covered his face with a towel and screamed.

"Jackson," Claire hissed. Jackson didn't look at her and tried to keep his face perfectly calm. He was in third period history, mostly not listening to his teacher talk about the San Juan Island Pig War of 1859. Jackson felt lightheaded and just wanted to close his eyes.

Claire was sitting about three rows up from Jackson. Even when they were in the same class, Claire usually didn't sit next to him, but with some other girls. Now she kept turning in her chair and trying to get his attention.

She wanted to know about Macy. Jackson could practically read her thoughts like they had popped out of her head and turned into those little comic strip bubbles. Jackson had been avoiding Claire all period—keeping his eyes on his desk.

Someone had etched an eyeball about the size of

a quarter into the desk's surface, and it stared back at him.

Jackson thought how he couldn't wait to see Macy at lunch and ask her what to do, and then he remembered all over again that he wouldn't see Macy. Not ever. It wasn't that he forgot she was dead. It was that he forgot she wasn't also alive. Like she could be both at the same time.

"Jackson," Claire said again, giving him a little wave. The teacher had probably noticed that Claire was talking, but Claire could get away with anything.

"What?" he hissed back, trying to imagine how he would normally sound. Kinda pissed off, most likely. Jackson had been a dick to his friends since his mom died.

Was Claire even really his friend? Or was Claire just Macy's friend who put up with him?

Claire sighed like she was some fucking martyr.

"Fine," she whispered. "After class." Then she turned back around. He saw her take out her phone and start texting below the desk. She was probably texting Macy, Jackson realized, and the pit in his stomach grew even deeper. He wondered what they had done with Macy's phone.

The bell rang, finally, and Jackson pushed his way out of the classroom. He thought he had out-distanced Claire, but then he felt her sharp little fingers dig into his arm.

"Wait a sec," she said.

"What?" Jackson leaned against the wall. He blinked and saw the red line growing across Macy's neck again. That's what happened almost every time he closed his eyes.

"I can't find Macy. She won't answer her phone." Claire was wearing a pair of big dangly earrings that Jackson particularly hated. They were Smurf-blue and made out of feathers or some shit. He kept looking at the ugly earrings, so he didn't have to meet her eyes when she asked, "Did you both stay at Trev's last night?"

When he didn't say anything, Claire punched

him in the arm. "Are you still drunk? Or does fucking Sam make you go deaf?" Now she was grinning, at least.

Jackson made himself laugh. "Sorry, just thinking about last night." That was the truth at least.

"So," Claire continued, "have you seen Macy? You have English with her, right? First period? Last time I saw her, she was sneaking up to Dom's room. If she doesn't tell me what happened soon, I'm going to have to start making things up. First, Dom takes off Macy's cape—slowly—sliding the silky red fabric down her trembling back . . . "

"Gross." Jackson put his hands over his ears and started walking away. "TMI." He felt nauseous again, and his headache was worse than ever. Maybe he had a migraine.

His mom used to get really bad headaches, before they knew she was really sick, and all she'd want to do was lie down in a dark room with a washcloth over her eyes. But Jackson didn't want to close his eyes because he just kept seeing Macy die—over and over again.

Claire smiled, probably not realizing that Jackson had never answered her question. "I guess I'll just find her at lunch. Tell her to text me, though, if you see her."

Jackson gave Claire a shaky thumbs up, then walked down the hall toward his next class. If he had eaten anything that morning, he would have thrown it up all over the kid in front of him. His headache felt like an extra heart pulsing in his temple. Maybe he could just go home sick, and no one would even notice.

Then he felt a hand on his arm. Sam.

"How're you doing?" she asked in a soft, un-Sam-like voice. She looked a lot better than he felt. Apparently, if you're Sam, you don't actually require sleep to look amazing. Just a shower and a change of clothes.

Her hair was still damp, and Jackson imagined water evaporating off her head and forming a cloud around them both. He could almost taste her shampoo—something spicy, like tea tree oil. Fuck, he needed sleep.

"I'm here. That's about all I can say." Jackson wanted to curl up on the hallway floor and lay his head on her shoes. He wanted to sleep. But if he slept, he didn't want to wake up again.

After his mom died, whenever he woke up he'd forget—just for a moment—that she was dead. Remembering again was fucking terrible. But this—Macy's blood pulsing through his hands—this memory was so much worse. He wanted to forget, forever. He wanted to hack out the piece of his brain that held Macy dying and throw it in a garbage disposal. He wanted some of that *Eternal Sunshine* shit that wiped your brain clean.

Sam was in his next class, calculus. She walked him to a desk in the back of the room and sat beside him, even though she usually made a point of sitting by herself over by the window. All through class, she kept glancing over at him. She didn't smile or anything like that. It was like she just wanted to make sure Jackson hadn't oozed out of his chair into a sloppy pile of grief all over the floor.

The other students' bodies seemed to vibrate in their chairs like a swarm of flies. Jackson hadn't noticed before how much noise people make. Even Sam breathed loudly where she sat beside him, and she kept tapping her pencil on her binder. *Tap, tap, tap.*

He started to feel sick again—really, really sick.

Jackson got up, interrupting the teacher with the loud scrape of his chair. He didn't wait to ask if he could go, but ran for it—one hand covering his mouth. Jackson didn't quite make it in time. Thin, hot bile pooled in his hand as he pushed open the guy's bathroom.

He retched in one of the stalls, his empty stomach churning. In between dry heaves, Jackson let his cheek rest on the cold rim of the toilet. Even after his body finally stopped trying to turn itself inside out, Jackson sat on the bathroom floor. As he stared into the toilet—the water cloudy with his own sick—Jackson thought how this was only the first day.

How was he going to get through a lifetime of this?

Chapter Two

When Sam got home from school she grabbed her pack of cigarettes off the kitchen counter and went out to the backyard. Her hands were shaking so badly that it took several tries to flick a flame out of the lighter.

Sam had five unanswered texts from Gregory. She had been ignoring them because—fuck—everything that had just happened, but the latest text read, *should I come out there?*

Sam texted back immediately. *I've got it covered.* She should have waited a few more minutes so it wasn't as completely obvious that she had been ignoring his other texts.

She paced in the backyard, trying to decide if she needed another cigarette. Yes. She did. After shaking another cancer stick (Trev's words) out of the pack, she struggled, again, to light it with her almost empty Bic. It just kept sparking with no flame, and the metal roller was soon so hot to the touch that it burned her thumb. She inhaled deeply on the cigarette, then sucked on her scalded thumb—exhaling smoke around her knuckles.

Fucking Gregory. The last thing Sam needed was Gregory showing up. She hadn't seen Trev's ex-boyfriend since they basically abandoned him in Texas a few months earlier. Trev didn't know that Sam was still in contact with him. He would be so pissed if he knew.

Sam didn't really know what their big breakup had been about, but Trev basically never wanted to see Gregory again. He'd get all prickly if she even mentioned his name. If Trev knew she had been texting Gregory all this time . . . well, she didn't really know what he'd do. It would probably involve a bathtub full of rum and Sam cleaning up his puke for a week.

Sam stared at the screen of her phone, waiting for another text to show up. When it started to ring, Sam almost dropped the phone into the weedy grass.

"Hello?" Sam answered, trying to sound calm. She watched the end of her cigarette slowly turn to cinders.

"Sam?" Fucking Gregory. He called *her*. Like he didn't know her voice. She recognized his voice immediately: deep, a little raspy. Gregory could have been a rock star with that voice. Maybe. In another life.

"Yeah, it's me. How are you? How's Texas?" Sam tried to sound chipper, but it came out a bit more sarcastic than intended.

There was a sigh. "Well, that's part of the reason I'm calling. I'm not in Texas anymore."

Shit. "Oh?" Chipper. Flight attendant-happy. "Back in New York then?"

"New Mexico. Just a short stop—I'm actually on my way out there. To Grey Hills."

"Oh?" Sam said again. After taking another drag off her cigarette, she breathed smoke out through her gritted teeth. She probably looked like a dragon.

Sam turned her face up toward the sky. Clouds were gathering—it might snow any day. Any second, really.

Gregory kept talking. "I should be there in about ten days, maybe less. I need to check in with a few people, but then I'm all yours."

"Oh, well, I'm not sure if this is the best timing," Sam said. "We're kinda about to move on ourselves."

Sam glanced up at one of the upper windows—Dom's room. She thought she saw a movement against the dark of the glass, but she wasn't sure. Dom hadn't gone to school that day, and Trev had stayed home too in case Dom fucking exploded or something. Not quite suicide watch, but close.

Sam wanted to stay home and sleep but she had been on Jackson duty. The Moss siblings to the rescue once again.

"Really?" Gregory said. "I thought some big things were happening there. The Fire? The Door?"

"Well . . . " Sam shouldn't have answered the phone. If she hadn't picked up, then she wouldn't have to lie to Gregory now, and to Trev later. Trev would *kill* her if he found out. "It's just that the Door thing didn't really pan out. It was a dead end."

Sam swallowed a mouthful of smoky spit at the word *dead* and tried not to cough into the phone. As she clenched and unclenched her hand against the plastic of her phone, Sam could still feel the heft of Macy's dead legs.

Sam knew that Gregory was frowning. When he frowned he stopped talking, like his thoughts were so fucking deep that he couldn't move his mouth at the same time. It was actually pretty endearing in person—Sam could totally see why her brother had hooked up with him. But on the phone it was a pain in the ass. "Gregory? Still there?"

"Yeah, still here," he said in his slow, deep voice. "I'm just wondering what you're planning this time, Mattie, and if you're ever going to let me in on it."

Sam's face burned. She hated it when Gregory used her real name. It was like he had reached a hand out from her past and wrapped it around her throat. She blinked back tears. She was too fucking tired for this.

"I go by *Sam* now, remember? And I'm not planning anything. I just don't know if it's a good idea for you and Trev to, you know, be around each other. It might still be too soon." That wasn't even a complete lie. It was actually probably one of the truest things that Sam had said to Gregory in a long time.

"Trev is a big boy. I'm sure he can deal with it. I'll see you in about a week, okay Sam?"

"Sure," Sam said as she shook her head and

stamped her cigarette into the grass. After he hung up, Sam closed her eyes and wondered how many heartbeats you could fit into a week. How many cigarettes.

Somewhere between too many and not fucking enough.

Chapter Three

When Jackson got home from school, he went straight to his room. He didn't stop to get his usual after-school snack of two blueberry Pop-Tarts (uncooked, right out of the little foil sleeve) and a can of Coke. His dad wasn't home from work yet, and Jackson needed just a few hours of quiet.

Sam and Trev had told him that they probably had one day until Macy's parents would realize that something was really wrong. One full day until they called the police. If it hadn't been for the other recent deaths, the police would probably treat her disappearance like any other teen runaway. But people had been dying in Grey Hills, and a missing girl would take top priority.

Jackson lay on his bed for a few minutes, holding his hands over his closed eyes until he saw tiny points of light. He was just starting to drift off to sleep when his phone buzzed in his pocket. He had a text from Macy's mom: *Is Macy with you?*

A few minutes later he got a text from Claire: *Where is Macy?* Then another from Claire: *Her mom is worried.*

Jackson couldn't think of how to answer. Instead, he pressed Sam's number, then waited as it rang. He slid onto the floor until he was hidden from the windows by his bed. It was stupid, but he felt safer there. Less exposed. When he got Sam's voicemail, he hung up and almost threw his phone across the room.

Was it cruel to let Macy's parents, and Claire—and every other person who cared about her—go on thinking that she was alive? Or was it kind?

Jackson would give anything to be where Macy's mom and dad were now—still in the *before*. *Before* they knew that something was seriously wrong. *Before* their hearts were broken all over again, just after losing their son.

Before was better in every way.

Jackson wished he had a time machine, something with buttons he could press and levers he could pull that would make this nightmare go away. A *Doctor Who* Tardis that could erase the entire last fucking year. But even if he could persuade himself that it was kinder not to tell them yet, her parents still deserved to know at some point, didn't they? He still had to tell them what happened to Macy, right?

His head was throbbing again, and he knew he had to lie down soon or he would probably pass out. Instead he dialed another number. It rang seven times before someone picked up.

"Grey Hills Gazette, how may I help you?"

"Hey," Jackson said, pressing his hand over his eyes. "Can I talk to my dad?"

~~~

"Tell me everything." His dad spoke slowly and, it seemed to Jackson, cautiously.

Jackson and his dad were in the kitchen. His dad had opened a beer and set it in the middle of the table. Jackson wasn't sure if the beer was for his dad or for him. Neither one of them reached for it.

Jackson closed his eyes and pressed his fingers to his temples. It just made his head feel worse. "I don't know where to start," he murmured.

"The beginning is usually a good place." Jackson's dad, Frank Cooper, had always been a quiet man and had only grown more reserved after his wife passed away. He had thinning blond hair and Jackson's nose. It was easy to see what Jackson's face would grow into in another thirty years.

When Jackson called the newspaper where his dad worked, he hadn't been certain that his dad would leave work early. He was always working lately.

Jackson nodded, but still didn't know what to say. Should he tell his dad everything? Even the stuff that Jackson himself hadn't really been able to see? Were the ghosts his secret to tell? Besides, he really couldn't fathom how to say those words out loud. He didn't think his mouth could do it.

"Macy's missing," Jackson finally said. The words sounded made up, like he was watching himself as an actor on a terrible TV show.

Jackson's dad frowned. "Missing? Since when?"

"Last night."

"Do her parents know?" Jackson could see his

dad's eyes dart to the phone on the kitchen counter.

"Yeah. I think so. They don't know where she is."

"But you do? Is that what you're trying to tell me?" Jackson's dad asked in his quiet voice. When Jackson didn't meet his eyes, his dad reached out and took hold of his son's chin, making him look up. "Do you know something?"

"Nothing. I don't know where she is." Everything Jackson said was true, but not really the truth. Jackson pulled his face away and looked down at his hands. The raw spot by his thumb had started to scab over, and he resisted the urge to pick at it again.

He didn't know why he thought it would help to talk to his dad. At the time it seemed like the only thing that would keep him from melting into floorboards. But it wasn't like his dad had been able to do a damn thing to keep his mother alive. What exactly had Jackson expected?

"Son. If Macy's mixed up in something dangerous—if she ran away—you need to tell me. Look, I know she's your friend, and you want to keep her secret, but you're not protecting her. If you know something, and you don't speak up, your silence could hurt her. Do you understand what I'm saying?"

Jackson's throat was too full to speak. He had known Macy was meeting someone in the woods—a ghost—and he had said nothing. He'd just followed her, as though he could actually *do* something. As though he could protect her. How fucking arrogant.

Macy is dead. Her body is dead and rotting somewhere, and I have no idea where she is. I don't know where she is, and I don't know what to do. Tell me what to do. Those were the words Jackson wanted to say to his dad.

He wanted the past twenty-four hours to spill

out of his head onto the table so his dad could see it—could examine everything that was chewing on his son's heart. But Jackson couldn't form the words. He couldn't say them out loud. He could barely think them.

"I don't know where she is," Jackson said again, because that was, truly, the only thing he knew for sure.

His dad narrowed his eyes, then reached for the beer. He took a quick swallow, then handed it to Jackson. Jackson took the beer but didn't drink any. He held it in both hands and picked at the label as the bottle sweated.

"I trust you," Jackson's dad finally said, after a long silence. "I trust you to do the right thing here. If you hear from Macy, do you promise me you'll tell someone? That you'll tell me?"

Jackson nodded, even though he knew that wasn't a promise he could keep. Because, if he did hear from Macy, that would either mean that he was going crazy or her ghost had come back to talk to him.

Or both, he supposed. And fuck if he was going to tell his dad any of that.

Chapter Four

Sam waited a few days before she told Dominick about Gregory's call. It wasn't that she didn't want to tell him . . . okay, that was exactly what it was. Once she told Dom that Gregory was on his way, Sam would have to make a decision. *Stay or go. Tell her brother or keep silent.*

What finally pushed her over the edge was a text from Gregory: *U still in GH? B there in 1 week.*

Sam hated Gregory's texts, with their lazy, incomplete words. He had unlimited text messaging, Sam was one hundred percent sure, so why not just write the word *you* or *be*? And was it so hard to type a fucking apostrophe?

But that wasn't the point. The point was that Sam was running out of time, and she still didn't have a plan. And if there was one thing that Dom was good at, it was making plans.

If Dom hadn't already slit his wrists in there (a distinct possibility, since he never left his room anymore), then he was definitely typing away on his computer, researching their next steps. Sam needed to know what that step was, and how Jackson would fit into it. She was not going to leave him behind, no matter what Dom wanted.

Sam knocked on Dom's door, but of course there was no answer. She knew he was in there. He hadn't come down to dinner (pizza, again . . . Sam was so sick of pizza. Why couldn't Trev learn to cook?), and Sam had heard him pacing around in his room. The joys of an old creaky house. Sam had chosen one of the downstairs rooms, and she could hear Trev and Dominick clomping around up there all the time.

She knocked again, and then tried the handle. Locked. Sam wanted to kick the door down. Sam could just imagine how the wood would crack and splinter and how perfect that would be because all Sam wanted to do was break something. Instead she pressed her hand flat against the door.

"Dom?" Sam could almost feel his anger vibrating through the wood. "We need to talk."

No answer.

"Dom. You do realize that I have the master key, right? I don't even need to pick the lock, which I could certainly do. I just need to go downstairs to the drawer in the kitchen, where the realtor left the keys and the manual for the fucking microwave, and I can unlock your door. Is that what you want? Or you can unlock your door now, and we can have this fucking conversation face to face right now."

Sam heard a sigh, and then footsteps. There was a muffled click, and then the door opened. She stepped into Dom's room, bracing herself for what she would see.

Dom's room was clean, and his bed was made. His window was wide open, and the air was so cold that Sam almost took a step back. Instead, she walked across the room and slammed the window shut.

"What do you want?" Dom asked. His face was almost perfectly expressionless. He looked like something that had been broken into so many pieces that you had to just throw it away and start over—a brand new Dominick Vega. A blank slate.

Sam knew that expression. It was one she often saw in the mirror.

"Gregory called me," Sam said, trying not to look at Dom. Instead, Sam ran her hand along the wet surface of the windowsill. A few drops of rain must have blown in before she closed the window. Sam wondered if the water would stain the wood.

"When?" he asked with his strangely flat voice.

"A few days ago." Sam took a seat at Dom's desk, tapping her fingers on the closed lid of his laptop. He frowned, but didn't ask her to move. "He said he's coming here."

Dom's frown turned into a scowl at that news. He lifted his hand like he wanted to throw something across the room, but his hand was empty so he just let it drop down at his side again. "Here?" he finally whispered. "Here as in Grey Hills?"

Sam nodded. "He wants to check up on us."

"Because of the Door."

"Of course."

Dom sighed and sat down on the edge of the bed. He covered his eyes with his hand. "Does Trev know?"

"Of course not," Sam said. It had been Dom's idea, after all, to keep their communication with Gregory a secret from Trev. At least, at first.

Sam and Dom both knew exactly how Trev

would react if he knew that they were feeding Gregory information about the Doors. After the way they had all left things in Texas, Trev would lose his fucking mind.

Sam tried to meet Dominick's eyes, but only managed to look above his right shoulder, toward a dark spot on the wall. He was looking down at his hands.

"Dom," she said, "I didn't tell Gregory anything. Not yet."

"He doesn't know about . . . "

"I didn't mention Macy, or the Door. I don't know if we should tell him. I don't even know if we should be here when he gets to town. We should probably have left already. Yesterday."

Someone was going to find Macy sooner or later, and then who knew what kind of evidence would be all over her body. Sam had no intention of going to jail. *Like father, like daughter . . .*

Dom nodded, still not looking at Sam. The

room, Sam noticed, was growing stuffy, and she now wished she hadn't closed the window. There was a smell to the room—a slightly sour tang that she couldn't quite identify. *Is that what grief smells like?* Sam thought idly, before realizing that it was death she was smelling. Rot.

Sam narrowed her eyes at Dom. "What have you been doing up here?"

Dom's face jerked up, and he finally met her eyes. After a too long pause, he said "I don't know what you mean."

"What's that smell?" The thing about Dom was that he couldn't lie, not to Sam. He could fail to mention things or change the subject, but he couldn't actually tell a lie without it showing all over his face. Not like Sam. She had learned how to wear her lies until they became part of her DNA.

Dom stood up. "We're done here." His face was turning red.

Sam almost clapped her hands. How adorable.

Dom actually thought he could hide something from her. Something big, she was suddenly certain. Before Dom could take a step toward her, Sam turned in the chair until she was facing the desk and flipped opened the laptop.

"Don't touch that—" Dom began, but it was too late. One look at the screen was all Sam needed to know exactly what he was planning. *That poor, broken fool.*

The page was open to an article about how to strip flesh from bone.

Dom took the computer off the desk and closed the lid. "Get the fuck out of my room." His voice was somewhere between a whisper and a growl.

Sam stood up, hands on the edge of the desk. "If you're doing what I think you're doing . . . "

"None of your goddamn business. That's what I'm doing." He clutched the laptop tight against his chest like he was protecting it, like he could keep his secret from spilling out like it was Pandora's fucking box.

"If you're doing what I think you're doing," Sam repeated, "then you're going to need help."

Dom shook his head, over and over again. "I'm not doing anything." But his eyes were wide—so wide she could practically see through them to another Dom inside. That Dom—the one who lived inside his own head most of the time—that Dom was screaming. That Dom needed her help.

Sam walked closer to Dominick. "Where is it?" She tried to keep her voice soft, but she knew her words were going to slice through him no matter what. "Where did you hide her?"

Dom's head drooped. He almost let go of his computer, but Sam took it out of his hands and set it back on the desk. Dom sank to the floor, with his back against the bed. He wrapped his arms around his knees, setting his chin on his wrist.

"I thought I could bring her back," he whispered.

Sam knelt down beside him, draping her arm over his back. "I know," she said. Then, "Show me."

Dom reached under the bed and pulled out a shoebox. It looked like something a child would use to store baseball cards. When he opened the lid, Sam put her hand over her mouth. The smell . . .

Once, in Texas—when they were still with Gregory—Sam had stumbled across a dead cat in an alley. She had been following the ghost of a dead junkie. Just when Sam was about to stab a knife into her neck, the ghost had given Sam the finger and walked right through a brick wall.

Sam had stepped backward, wondering if she should try to climb the wall somehow—maybe stack some boxes on top of the trash bin—when her foot landed on something soft. She had stepped on a cat. It had been dead for a few days at least, and Sam's heel had torn a hole right through the cat's stomach. The smell that came out of the cat was enough to make her gag.

The cat's mouth was slightly open, Sam remembered, and its eyes were gone. And to make that fucking day even worse, Sam never did catch the ghost.

A whisper of that same smell—cloying and thick and somehow sweet—emerged from the shoebox.

"What is it?" Sam whispered. She thought she'd be able to look, but she couldn't. She had to close her eyes against the smell.

Sam could hear a small scrape of cardboard. Dom had closed the lid. It didn't really make the smell better, but she was able to open her eyes.

Dom whispered something, but Sam couldn't quite hear.

"What?" she asked. She edged slightly away from him instead of leaning closer. The metal frame of the bed dug into her back. The reality of the box was starting to sink in. Dom must have gone back there—after. He must have dug her up . . .

"A finger," Dom whispered, this time loud enough for Sam to hear.

Sam closed her eyes again. One of her hands was still resting on Dom's back. She could feel the rise and fall of his breathing all the way up her arm. She reached back with her other hand, as though trying to find something solid to hold onto. Her hand only found the dusty wood floor under the bed.

"Her finger," Sam echoed back, swallowing. "And . . . her hair?"

"A little bit. Not much. Just a few strands."

And Dom would have had plenty of her blood already, from Jackson's clothes. From all of their clothes, really. Dom had volunteered to dispose of them. She hadn't even suspected that he had something else in mind.

Sam dug her nail into a line between the floorboards. She was back there, in the woods, carrying Macy's legs. Trev had Macy's shoulders and was going first. Dom held the flashlight. Macy had tights that caught the moonlight, giving off a ghostly shimmer.

Sam remembered thinking those words exactly, *ghostly shimmer*, like she was in a fucking novel, and not tripping over blackberry vines and almost blinding herself on tree branches that whipped back into her face when her brother let go of them.

"How far did you get?" Sam asked, struggling to keep her voice calm. Her free hand moved to another floorboard, and she ran her nail up the seam. Maybe she was turning into one of those OCD people who had to count the lines in the floors and the cracks in the walls.

Dom shrugged Sam's hand off his back. She pulled that hand away and tugged on the end of her hair, wrapping it around her fingers.

"Not far. It's the skin. I didn't . . . it's just that I didn't think it would be like that."

Sam was trying to think of what she could possibly say when something bit her finger. At least, that's what it felt like. She had been sliding it along the crack of another floorboard when something sharp stabbed into the tip of her pointer finger. She ripped her hand back, imagining a rat had just sunk it's fangs into her hand and had injected her with rabies or something.

"Mother fuck!" Sam hissed, looking at her injured finger. A dark bead of blood welled up from around a huge splinter. It was almost cartoonishly big, with the dark shadow of the tip sticking in a good half inch beneath her skin.

Dom didn't set down the box, but he held out his hand. "Let me see." Dom wasn't usually the one to tend to wounds. That was Trev.

Trev had a doctor's hands. Her brother was the one who had held Sam's bleeding arm together after those ghosts in New Mexico sliced her up. Dom had taken out those two ghosts, one right after the other, while Trev held his shirt over her wound.

But now Sam let Dom hold her finger still and pull the splinter free. It felt like the only thing she could give him.

"Ow!" Sam took her hand back once he was done and put her finger in her mouth. Her blood tasted like batteries. Then she pulled out her phone and set it to a flashlight app. She shined it under the bed.

"What're you doing?" Dom asked. He got up and threw the bloody splinter into the trash. He was so fucking tidy. Sam's room, on the other hand, looked like the inside of a hobo's shopping cart.

"I'm finding the bastard that stabbed me." She waved the light around, looking for a rough snag of wood. There, about a foot beneath the bed, was a cracked board. She could see a line right up center of it. "Old fucking house," she muttered. She turned off the flashlight, but then, right before she looked away, Sam realized she could still see the crack in the board. There was a light shining through it, up from beneath the floor. A soft, blue light.

"Is your bedroom above the kitchen? I think I can see through."

"What?"

"There's a light shining through your floor. This house is so shitty."

Dom kneeled down. "There should be insulation between. You shouldn't be able to just see through to the first floor."

Sam scooted back. "The ceiling is so thin, man. I can hear every step you and Trev make. You're like baby elephants."

"What on earth . . . " Dom reached his hand down under the bed. "It's definitely a light . . . Gimme your flashlight, I want to look at the board."

"I just have my phone." Sam didn't really want to just hand Dom her phone. Her phone was private. Anyway, her finger was really throbbing. She probably needed some kind of antiseptic to get rid of all the *under-Dom's-bed* germs.

"Okay, then give me your fucking phone," Dom snapped. He held out his hand, but Sam shook her head.

"Just move your bed."

Dom looked like he was going to argue with her for a moment, but then shrugged.

Together they moved the bed away from the wall with a loud scraping sound. The blue light was clearly visible shining between the crack in the floorboard. "What on earth is it?" Sam asked.

Just then there was a knock at the door. "What are you guys doing up here? If that sound was you guys having kinky sex then I'm just ending it right now. I have a noose ready and everything."

Sam glanced at Dom. He nodded, then stowed the shoebox in his closet while Sam opened the door. "We found something weird," she said, pointing to the broken floorboard.

"Thank God," Trev said. Her brother still looked like hell, but at least he seemed freshly showered, and didn't smell like beer anymore. Then he said, "Wait. What'd ya mean weird?"

Dom went and got a hammer out of the basement, and then he and Trev pried up the cracked floorboard while Sam peered over her brother's shoulder.

When she saw what had been covered by the wooden board, she gasped. The light wasn't coming from the kitchen. It was a thin, blue, jagged line of light that seemed to weave through the air itself. Like a worm, Sam suddenly thought. A big, fat glowworm that had burrowed into their house.

Sam rubbed her eyes. "You're both seeing this, right?" she said. The light was making her head swim.

Trev bent down to take a closer look. "Houses don't normally . . . glow, do they?"

Dom said, "There's something else in there." Before Sam could react Dom reached his hand into the hole in the floor.

"What the fuck, Dom!" she cried, but he was already pulling his arm back. In his hand was a very old-looking book. He flipped open the cover, then let out something like a laugh or a cough. Inside, in faded, spidery writing were the words: PROPERTY OF ELI GREY.

Chapter Five

"What'd you mean you're leaving?" Jackson tried to keep his voice down, but he couldn't control the edge of panic in his words. Trev and Sam were sitting with Jackson at lunch. Dom wasn't there—he hadn't been back to school since Halloween.

It was Friday, four days since Macy's "disappearance." That's the word the police had used when they talked to Jackson a few days earlier. That was the word everyone said when they tried not to say things like *killed* or *dead*.

The whole school was talking about her. There were so many different theories. Had Macy gone crazy after everything that happened (her brother's death and the school fire) and killed herself? Had she just run away? Or had she been murdered like that substitute teacher?

The police had arrested a man for the death of the substitute teacher before Macy vanished (a drifter who was found with the teacher's wallet). But what if they had the wrong man? What if a killer was still out there?

A few people had even started to look suspiciously at Jackson.

Across from Jackson at the lunch table, Trev was twisting the stem off his apple. "We're making like trees."

"What?" Jackson asked, poking at his uneaten food.

"Making like trees and leaving. That's how it goes, right?"

Sam threw a tater tot at her brother's head. "Sarcastic fuck."

Jackson shook his head. "You can't leave."

How could they even talk about it? As if they could just go have a normal life in a different town—like nothing had ever happened? Like Macy had never even existed?

"Jackson." Sam pressed her lips together. They turned slightly down at the corners. She looked like she was disappointed in him—as if she was a teacher, and he got a question wrong on a test. An easy one. "We're not just leaving. I mean, we are. But we want you to come with us."

"Dom doesn't," Trev volunteered. "Full disclosure. He wanted us to leave without telling you. So, FYI, you'll have to deal with his shit if you come with us. I think he needs therapy. But you probably do too, so maybe you could do some kind of a two-for-one session or something. Buy one get one free?"

"Bro, shut up." Sam aimed another tot at his head, but this time Trev caught it in his mouth.

Jackson shook his head. "Go where? I don't have any money. What would I even do? It's not like I can help you guys bust ghosts or whatever. I'm not like Macy."

It was true that Jackson couldn't see ghosts the way Macy had. But he had seen that one ghost— the boy who killed Macy. Jackson had watched him walk through the Door. Maybe Jackson *could* see other ghosts. That wasn't really the fucking point, was it? Even if he had the best damned ghost radar on the planet, was he just going to run away with a strange little band of ghost hunters? Just leave Grey Hills and his dad?

Jackson wished that he could ask Macy what to do.

"You don't need money." Trev said. "We've got plenty. Don't get me wrong, you'll have to pay your way in sexual favors, but that's our standard deal."

"Just your basic boilerplate," Sam added with a thin smile. Jackson missed Sam's real smile, he suddenly realized. The one where you could see too many of her teeth, and Sam looked like she might bite you in half. He hadn't seen her smile like that in a while.

"Even if I wanted to just . . . just run for it, what about the police? Isn't that going to look suspicious? They'd look for me, right? Wouldn't they just bring me back and assume I did it?" Jackson looked over his shoulder after he said that that last part. For the past few days he'd been super jumpy. It felt like someone was always standing right behind him. "I mean, they've already talked to me once. What if they already think I had something to do with her . . . disappearance?"

Sam took his hand. Jackson's stomach clenched. "You don't seem to understand what we're offering. You wouldn't be *Jackson Cooper* anymore. You wouldn't ever come back here. We'll give you a new identity. A fresh start."

While his sister was talking, Trev put the apple stem in his mouth, then made a face and spit it out again into the palm of his hand. "Witness protection program, Moss style," he said, gesturing at

Jackson with the soggy stem. "No expenses spared. We can even dye your hair. I'm thinking red."

⌐◡⌐

At the end of the day, when Jackson was leaving his final class, he walked past the trophy display. There, on a middle shelf, was a memorial to the two students who had died in the fire. There were pictures, cards, poems, and one stuffed bear that had belonged to Cassandra Decker.

Below the memorial was a second tribute to those who died in the Fire fifty years earlier. Newspaper clippings and a partially melted plaque that used to be some kind of sports award. Jackson could just make out a few letters and numbers. And there, beside the melted plaque, was a framed photograph of dead Principle Grey and his nephew.

Something about the photo drew Jackson's gaze. He leaned over to look closer. What was the nephew's name? Jackson should remember it, but when he tried to think of it his mind just went fuzzy. He had seen that picture before, he was pretty sure, but there was something about it . . . something familiar.

Jackson's head started to throb again, and he closed his eyes tight. That pounding in his head—would it ever go away?

While he stood, his face inches from the display glass, eyes closed, someone grabbed his arm. He opened his eyes, half-expecting to see Sam.

Claire's face stared up at him. "We need to talk," she said sharply, not breaking eye contact for a second.

She looked strange. It took him a moment to realize that she wasn't wearing any makeup. Claire almost looked like a different person without makeup—like a connect-the-dots drawing before someone took a pen to it.

He shrugged her off, taking a step back. "No. We really don't," he said a little too sharply. Jackson's head hurt too much to deal with Claire.

"Jackson fucking Cooper. You will not walk away from me." Claire was at least a full foot shorter than him, but standing there, hands at her sides—blocking Jackson's path—she looked like one of those Amazons from Greek mythology. The ones who cut off their boobs and killed men with arrows.

He let out a loud, exasperated sigh. "What? What could you possibly want?"

"What do I want? I want Macy back. I want her to answer her phone and let me know where she is. I want her to let me know that she's safe and happy and fucking alive.

"It's been four days, Jackson. Four fucking days. And you just come and go like it's no big deal? Like it doesn't even matter that your best friend is missing? What do I want? I want you to act like you're a fucking human being and not a robot. What's wrong with you, Jackson?"

"Nothing. I don't know." Jackson was sweating. He needed to get outside. He needed Claire to stop talking.

"Nothing. I don't know," Claire parroted back. "Something is seriously wrong with you, Jackson. Did something happen between you and Macy? She told me about that day in the basement, you know. She told me how you attacked her. Did you think she would just keep your little secret? How you practically tried to rape your best friend?"

Claire's voice filled the hall, and other students stopped and stared at them.

Jackson took a step toward her. Claire needed to lower her voice. Now. "You don't know anything about it. It wasn't like that."

"She had a bruise on her wrist, did you know that? Yeah. She showed me. Did you hurt her again? Did you do something to her? Did she run away?"

"Shut up!" Jackson took hold of Claire's shoulders. "That's not what happened! That's not . . . it wasn't like that."

Let her go, a soft voice seemed to whisper in Jackson's ear.

Did he just hear that? For an instant Jackson thought he was seeing double—one little blonde Claire staring up at him and a darker Claire standing right behind her. A shadow Claire. Jackson closed his eyes and shook his head. When he opened his eyes there was just one angry Claire glaring up at him.

Claire lowered her voice until only Jackson could hear her words. "If you don't take your hands off me, right now, I'll scream. And then I'll tell everyone I saw you follow Macy out of the Halloween party."

Chapter Six

Sam picked up the leather-bound book. She'd already read it twice. She turned to the first page again, as though it would reveal something she hadn't already seen. "Eli Grey, huh? Who the fuck are you?"

The leather binding felt dry—almost scaly—and she wished she was wearing gloves. Flipping through a few more pages, Sam once again admired the small, polite-looking black handwriting. So neat and even. The type of handwriting that would tip its hat as it walked by.

She read it out loud:

The cracks have always been there. I can hear them singing. The dead.

Only they aren't always songs. There are screams too, and weeping. And laughter. The kind of laughs that you only hear in a madhouse. It is the laughter that keeps me awake at night. Children's laughs. Women.

My father cannot hear the voices. They all think I am mad. Not just north-by-northwest mad, but truly mad. They think I might hurt them. But they have no idea. They have no concept of pain.

"And it just goes on like that," Dom said, "for like, a hundred pages." He held out his hand to take the book back from Sam.

"Shit . . . " Trev contributed. *Thanks, bro. So fucking helpful, as always.*

They were all sitting around the kitchen table after school on Friday, drinking coffee this time because Trev was going to get alcohol poisoning if he kept going like he had been the last few days and they all knew it. Sam wanted to invite Jackson to come check out the journal, but Dom didn't want them to tell Jackson, or anyone else, about the journal yet "just in case."

Sam knew that Dom just didn't want to be in the same room as Jackson. He really needed to just get over himself already. He was driving her crazy.

When they first saw Jackson holding Macy's body, Sam and Trev both had to hold Dom back. Sam didn't know what Dom would have done if her arm hadn't been wrapped around his throat. Something bad.

Dom still questioned Jackson's story, trying to poke holes in it. He said it didn't make sense that Jackson would suddenly be able to see the ghost who had killed Macy when he hadn't been able to see any other ghosts before. Sam was worried that, deep down, Dom still thought that Jackson had killed her himself.

While Sam and Dom read over the journal again, Trev was looking up stuff up on his phone—ancestry websites, local historical documents—but he hadn't found anything about an Eli Grey yet.

"I mean," Sam said, holding her cup of coffee beneath her face so the steam warmed her lips, "he has to be related to that principal—Richard Grey—right?"

Dom nodded, "Must be. And the nephew, Henry Grey, this was his house."

Sam rolled her eyes at the way Dom said that, like that was new information. "Yeah. I know." That was exactly why they bought this particular house in the first place.

Trev looked up from his phone. "No record of an Eli Grey owning this house. Just Alexander Grey. Henry's dad."

Dom added, "I'm just saying they have to be related somehow. Maybe the journal was a family heirloom or something."

Sam took a long sip of the coffee—black and a little too bitter. Then she said, "Who do you think Mabel was? And that last line . . . *Death*

is not the end—do you think he killed himself?"
Sam wished Gregory was with them. He always
seemed to know a bit more than the rest of them,
or he was just a bit quicker to piece things together. Gregory always knew the right questions
to ask.

"Mabel . . . " Trev said, typing away at his phone
again. "That name sounds familiar."

Sam knew she had to tell Trev soon that Gregory was on his way, but she still hadn't decided if
they were going to stick around long enough for
Gregory to catch up with them. She wished Trev
would just tell her why he hated Gregory so much
that they had moved halfway across the country to
avoid him.

The last time she had brought it up Trev had
told her to mind her own fucking business and
then had locked himself in his room for the rest of
the night.

Sam wanted to understand, because right now
she couldn't really imagine what could be such a

huge deal when they could really use Gregory's help. He'd know exactly what to do. She'd never forget Texas, and what Gregory had done for her. For all of them.

◦~◦

It was the night they met Gregory, about a year ago. The three of them were in a small town just outside Austin—still holed up in a hotel because they hadn't planned on staying for that long and hadn't gotten an apartment yet.

Dom was looking for a particular ghost. A woman who had been killing young men. A siren, Dom had called her, which Sam found too fucking romantic, like some sad-eyed painting of a mermaid. It always annoyed her when Dom came up with pet names for ghosts, like they were part of a collection he was keeping.

They were just ghosts, until they took care of them. And then they were nothing.

Apparently this ghost, this siren, would pick up men just outside of bars and then literally rip out their hearts. She would leave them bleeding in alleys or in dirty motel rooms. The police thought they had a serial killer on the loose. They weren't wrong . . .

Sam had her own room, and she spent most days marathoning episodes of the *Bachelorette* and *Game of Thrones*. They had driven from New Mexico two weeks earlier, and she was still healing from where the two ghosts had carved up her arm.

She didn't like to think about what they would have done to her if Dom hadn't come to her rescue like a knight in shining fucking armor—or how useless it made her feel.

Sam wouldn't admit it to the others, but she was terrified to go back out there. She was scared that it wouldn't matter how much she had practiced, or how strong she pretended she was. The ghosts could see right through to the gooey center of her—the mess that was still curled up on the floor of her parents' kitchen, watching blood collect in the lines of the tile floor.

After literally spending eight unmoving hours on the bed watching TV, Sam had decided to go with Trev and Dom to one of the bars they were staking out to look for the siren. They never carded Sam at those dive bars so she went right in ahead of Dom and Trev and started off the night with a few shots of Fireball. Disgusting stuff, but a guy at the bar was paying.

She started to not mind that much when another man called her Red and tried to dance with her. She forgot for a few moments how those ghosts in New Mexico had looked while they took turns licking her blood off the knife. They looked alive.

Sam didn't think that Dom was going to find his siren that night. He seemed to have given up too and was just chatting up some blonde in the corner. Sam had wondered, laughing to herself, if the blonde knew how completely underage Dominick was. Cradle-robber.

Fast forward an hour, and Sam had lost track of Dom. He had been talking to that girl, she remembered, but then what? She tried Dom's phone but no answer.

Trev was playing pool with some hot Asian guy. Hottie was wearing a shirt with the Stay Puft Marshmallow Man from the *Ghostbusters* movie on it. Trev must have just died when he saw that shirt.

Sam tried to get his attention, but Trev just made a face at her and went back to his game. So Sam had sauntered out the front door to look for Dom herself. When Sam was drunk she didn't wobble or stagger. She walked like a fucking lady.

Sam found Dom down a nearby alley, making out with that blonde. She had him pressed up against a wall, and it looked like they were really going at it. Sam had been about to turn around and go back in bar when she saw a second woman emerge from the shadows. This one was shorter, with pale, bare arms and long, dark hair.

The second woman shoved the blonde woman aside. That was when Sam saw that Dom was just leaning against the wall—ragdoll arms hanging at his side.

"Hey!" Sam called out, when a third woman appeared right in front of her. This woman had bright pink lipstick, and when she smiled in Sam's face, her teeth seemed to glow. "What—?" Sam had started to say when the new woman punched her in the face.

Sam dropped, clutching her bleeding nose and trying not to inhale her own blood. *Fuck!* Sam tried to stand up, but the third woman kicked her and then held her to the ground with a heel pressed to Sam's throat.

Sam watched as two more women—making five total—appeared as if from thin air. That was when she watched the first woman, the blonde, pull the dark-haired woman off Dominick. And then the blonde sank her hand into his chest. Sam stared up at the woman who had her pinned to the dirty cement, and she realized with either horror or relief—she couldn't tell which at the time—that she could see the orange glow of a nearby streetlight shining through her.

Ghosts. They were motherfucking ghosts. Five of them.

At least ghosts were something Sam knew how to deal with. Most of the time. The ghost woman stepped harder on her throat, and Sam couldn't breathe. She tried to reach for the knife at her belt, but she was starting to see huge, black spots swimming around her vision like she had stuck her head inside a lava lamp.

Sam tried to just use her mind—to focus on the outline of the woman above her, but she had never been any good at that. Not like Dom. She needed her knives.

She had scratched at the ghost's leg, but the woman just pressed down harder. Sam couldn't even see Dom anymore—she just saw the four other ghosts who were pushing and shoving each other and trying to grab at him.

The siren was never one ghost, Sam realized with one of her last coherent thoughts. They were *sirens*. How had Dom not known? More ghosts working together, like those two in New Mexico.

Shit. When had ghosts started to form gangs?

Sam kept kicking and scratching and trying to scream but it was no good. And the ghost just smiled and laughed above her. A terrible laugh. It was less a laugh than a bird of prey's cry. This woman, this ghost, was enjoying this. She liked to kill.

Just when Sam was sure that the black blobs in front of her eyes were going to consume her, Sam heard shouting. It sounded like her brother. And then there were screams—high, piercing screams. The ghost who was trying to kill her was screaming and burning. Her hair was on fire, and her skin was melting down her face. The ghost released her, and Sam rolled away, coughing and sucking in deep breathes. The whole alley was full of fire as the five ghosts burned and screamed like their very souls were being ripped apart.

Maybe they were. Maybe that was exactly what they did to the ghosts when they "took care" of them. And there, standing at the mouth of the alley was Gregory. Only she didn't know him as Gregory yet. He was the hot guy Trev had been playing pool with . . . wearing a motherfucking *Ghostbusters* T-shirt.

With his arms raised, and glowing in the reflected light of the burning ghosts, Gregory looked like a god. In those moments, while Sam lay coughing and sputtering, she thought he was the most beautiful thing she had ever seen.

❧

As Sam stared at the journal in Dom's hands, she wondered if it was time to just let Gregory take care of all this. Sam looked across the table to her brother, who was still swiping at this phone.

She took a long sip of her coffee. It was already cold.

Chapter Seven

On Friday night, Jackson woke up in the middle of a movie theater. Jackson looked around. It was the Opal, which made sense because it was the only movie theater in this tiny-ass town.

The theater was about half-full, and a movie was already playing. Some kind of action film, with explosions that sounded like thunder.

He blinked, and shook his head as though that simple act could clear away the fog that lingered in the corners of his vision. Jackson wasn't sure when the sleepwalking had started. Two days ago he had woken up halfway down the stairs, with his right hand clutching the railing and his left foot raised, about to take another step. He had almost tumbled the rest of the way down the stairs when he found himself like that, but he managed to keep his balance.

Jackson pulled his phone out of his pocket and turned on the screen, angling it down so hopefully no one would notice the light. Eight-thirty p.m. There was no way in hell Jackson had already been asleep that early. Was it still sleepwalking if you weren't even asleep to start with?

But that wasn't even the point, was it? How on God's fucking green earth could Jackson have sleepwalked out of his house, walked the mile or so downtown, and purchased his ticket—all while fast asleep?

Maybe he was suffering from short-term memory loss. Jackson had heard about that happening to people who suffered head injuries or traumatic experience.

At least, he heard it on that movie, *Memento*, about a dude who couldn't remember shit for more than, like, a few hours at a time. In the movie, the main character was trying to track down his wife's killers, but had to tattoo all of his clues onto his body because he just forgot everything right after it happened. Macy had been obsessed with that movie in eighth grade so Jackson had watched it about ten times in a three-month span.

Maybe that's what was happening to Jackson now. Maybe he had some kind of amnesia.

Jackson closed his eyes again, gripping the arms of the theater chair like it was the captain's chair of the fucking Starship Enterprise and they had just entered warp speed. That's what his life felt like lately—everything was just zooming past him, and he couldn't make it slow down. For several minutes Jackson just watched the flicker of the movie on the back of his eyelids.

He needed to talk to Sam. And Trev and Dominick, probably, but mostly Sam. She was the only one who actually seemed to listen to him. Maybe he *should* just pack up and leave with them.

Maybe all he needed was to get the hell out of this town and leave all these memories behind, like so many stars whipping past.

It wasn't like he cared if he ever saw anyone from Grey Hills again. Claire, for one, could go fuck herself. How dare she say those things to him at school? How dare she even think that he would hurt Macy? But his dad, Jackson remembered. He couldn't just leave his dad. Or could he?

Maybe his dad would be better off if Jackson was gone. Maybe he could just start over. Have a new wife. A new family. That happened all the time. People could just start again.

Maybe Jackson could start again. With Sam.

Someone touched his right hand. Jackson's eyes snapped open, but he didn't move. There, sitting next to him, was a woman with dark hair and a profile like a 1920's movie star.

Was she . . . ? He tried to look closer without letting on that he was staring. Macy had told him about the ghost in the movie theater. They had even gone back there once or twice, but Macy never did find her again. They thought that one of the twins must have taken care of her already.

The woman was watching the movie, and she flinched during the next big explosion. Jackson was pretty sure he could see the ball of fire from the movie reflected in her eyes. Her hand felt solid and very dry. Her skin reminded him of how a moth's wing *looked* like it would feel.

"Hello?" Jackson whispered, tilting his head ever so slightly in her direction. The woman seemed to ignore him at first, or maybe she just didn't hear him. Then she turned away from the film—reluctantly, Jackson thought—and met his eyes. Or rather, she looked somewhere just beyond his eyes. It felt like she was looking right through him into the middle of his skull.

"Hello," she said. She had a sweet voice—that was the word for it. Light, and almost childish. Smooth like chamomile tea with a few drops of honey. Is that what ghosts sounded like? The woman looked down at their hands and sort of frowned, then removed her hand and set it in her lap.

"I'm Jackson," he whispered.

She nodded. "Yes." It was a strange nod—not like she was learning his name, but like she was giving him permission to *be* Jackson. "You're Jackson. I can see that now."

"Did you think I was someone else?" This should have all been a dream, but he knew it wasn't. Sometimes Jackson had dreams where he thought he was awake, but he had never thought he was dreaming when he was actually awake. Reality was too specific. He could feel the sticky residue of spilled pop under his shoes, and there was a small crack in the armrest that he had started to pick at with his thumbnail.

"No," the woman replied. "You *were* someone else."

Jackson realized that he still didn't know if she was just a really eccentric *living* woman or the ghost. Not for sure. And that wasn't something you could just come out and ask. *Excuse me, Ma'am. Are you a ghost?* He tried to see if the light from the movie would shine through her the way Macy had described, but he couldn't tell.

It turned out that Jackson didn't have to ask. The woman vanished. Jackson immediately reached over and set his hand on the empty seat. It was cool to the touch—not like a person had just been sitting there.

He shivered once, violently. *Someone walking over his grave.* Wasn't that the expression?

Jackson wondered if he should leave or watch the rest of the movie. He had, presumably, paid for it after all. Now it looked like some kind of a spy film, though he didn't recognize any of the actors so far. Someone was tied to a chair.

A hand touched his arm. She was back and seemed to look at him shyly in the dim light— only half-turning toward him. Or, he realized, she didn't want him to see the gunshot wound on the other side of her head. Macy had told him about that, too.

"I hate this movie," the woman whispered. "Too violent."

"Why are you watching it?" Jackson asked, glancing at her out of the corner of his eye. Her hand was so pale it almost looked green.

She shrugged. "I've seen it fourteen times so far. What else is there to do?" For a moment he thought she was making some kind of weird afterlife joke, but she wasn't smiling.

Shit. What *was* there to do after you died? What would Jackson do if he was a ghost? Probably sit around watching movies with Macy's ghost. *If* Macy was a ghost . . .

Jackson wasn't sure which he should be hoping for—that she was a ghost or that she had moved on to wherever you were really supposed to go after you die. A good person would *not* hope that his best friend was a ghost, but Jackson wasn't sure how *good* he really was.

Jackson took a chance and softly asked, "What's your name?"

"Mabel." Something about her honey-sweet voice made him uncomfortable, and he tried not to squirm in his chair.

"Do you know why I'm here?" Jackson asked. He wished Sam were here. But Sam would probably just scare Mabel away. Or make her disappear for good. Which, Jackson considered, might not be the worst idea. Why should he care if this ghost was destroyed? Isn't that what they were supposed to do with ghosts? If Macy had just destroyed that ghost by the Door, she would still be alive.

But there was also this feeling—an itchy, antsy sensation, almost like déjà vu—when he heard Mabel's voice. Almost like he knew her.

The ghost didn't speak for a moment, and Jackson wasn't even sure if she had understood his question. What happened to your brain when you became a ghost? Was it all cobwebs and dust? Just an empty room filled with shadows?

Then she said, "You're here because of a debt. You owe me."

"What?" Jackson realized that her hand was still gripping his arm. It almost hurt, but at the same time he wasn't sure if he could actually feel the pressure of her fingers. It wasn't like a real hand, he decided. It was the memory of a hand.

"Sorry. Not you. It was someone else. He looks like you now."

The woman turned then and placed her other hand on his face—making him look at her. "You shouldn't come here anymore. I don't want you to come here." Her cool fingers dug into his cheek, and hooked along his jaw. "You need to let me go now. I don't want you here."

There was a thin trickle of blood just below her right ear. Seeing the wound on her head felt too intimate, like seeing her naked. He tried to just look at her eyes.

"I'll go," Jackson whispered. Her eyes were so dark that there was no bottom to them. Jackson was so close to her face that he could see his reflection in her eyes. No . . . it wasn't *his* face. It was another face. A man with dark hair. The man in the ghost's eyes was frowning.

Then Jackson heard himself say, "No."

Jackson definitely didn't say that. At least, he didn't mean to. When he spoke again, the words felt like they were being said with air forced out of his lungs—as though someone was squeezing his chest. "It wasn't supposed to be like this. You were supposed to be with me."

Mabel looked away first, pushing Jackson's face away from her. "That was never going to happen. Let the poor boy go." Her eyes filled with tears, and she dabbed her eyes with the edge of her sleeve. He had time to wonder why she dried her tears with her sleeve and not the trickle of blood (and how did ghosts cry anyway?), when he felt a sharp, stabbing pain in his left temple. It didn't feel like a headache anymore, but a fucking bomb in his head.

"I'm stronger now. But you don't care about that, do you, darling?" Jackson heard himself spit out—his words dripping with poison. "You thought you'd gotten rid of me, didn't you? That you could take daddy's gun and shoot me out of your head?"

"You owe me," Mabel said in a shaky voice. She even seemed to flicker slightly, and Jackson could see what Macy had described as the light from the movie filtered through her body. "You took away my life. My whole life. You owe me a life."

"You're just a stupid bitch. You're a stupid, dead bitch. I don't know why I keep coming back here. Stupid. Dead. Bitch."

She shook her head and covered her face with her hands. Then she turned to Jackson again and set her fingers back on the side of his head—right where his temple was pounding.

Where her fingers touched him this time, it tingled like a limb falling asleep. And then she sank her fingers into his brain. He froze—Jackson didn't know how he knew that her fingers were inside his skull, but he could clearly picture her hand ending at the knuckles, sticking out of the side of his head.

He couldn't speak, or even breathe. All he could do was watch her lips as she—finally—smiled. She looked more alive when she smiled.

"Eli. I can see you, did you know that? I can still see you in there. You look ugly."

Jackson was trembling, and then that tingling sensation spread outwards from his head—down the back of his neck and radiating out into his limbs. The tips of his fingers felt electric.

Then, he had his hands on Mabel's neck. His hands were glowing. "Look at what you're making me do, darling. I don't want to do this."

She shook her head, clawing at his arms, letting out a weak whimper, and then a sigh. She stopped fighting and gave him a sad look. A disappointed look.

And then she was gone again.

Jackson looked down at his glowing hands. He

could see the bones of his fingers—the long, thin lines where they ran down the back of his hand and joined at the wrists. When he looked at his palms, a bright, wavering light shimmered across his skin. It didn't feel hot, like fire. And it didn't feel cold. It felt like nothing—like his own blood. Jackson tried to remember where he had seen a light like that before, because it seemed too familiar.

The light danced across his hands and licked up his arms. Could the rest of the theater see him? Was he illuminated like the light from a cell phone? Was an usher going to come tell him to turn himself off?

Jackson started to laugh, but he wasn't sure if it was his laugh or not. He didn't feel like laughing. He didn't actually feel much at all. While he stared into the light, his mind still felt kind of tingly like where the ghost had touched him. It was as if his brain was jacked up on Novocain from the dentist office. Swimmingly, floating—numb.

He wasn't sure of anything, really, except that

he suddenly remembered what the light reminded him of. The last time he had seen that light, something else had been covering his hands. Macy's blood. The light looked exactly like the light of the Door. The same color or lack of color. The same undulating, wavering movement. Jackson felt like he was sinking underwater.

It felt glorious.

Chapter Eight

On Saturday Jackson slept until two p.m. It had been five days since Macy died. That was how Jackson kept track of the time now. Jackson didn't remember when he went to bed the night before, but it hadn't been that late. Why had he slept so long, and why did he still feel exhausted?

He remembered his dad knocking on his door around noon, but Jackson had just turned over in bed and ignored him. His dad was gone when Jackson finally got up. Frank Cooper didn't strictly need to go in on Saturday, so his absence just meant that he'd rather be at work than at home.

Jackson was going to make toast, but when he

took a slice of bread out of the bag he remembered how Macy used to just eat wadded-up pieces of bread as a snack. She was so weird.

Jackson balled up the piece of bread in his own fist but couldn't bring himself to eat it, so he tossed it in the garbage. He was about to just walk upstairs and go back to bed when the doorbell rang.

For an instant he thought it might be the police, and that they had found Macy's body. But then he heard Sam's muffled voice calling through the door. "Jackson? It's just me."

Jackson opened the door and there she was, bundled in a down jacket, her cheeks flushed red from the cold.

"You should come over to my house," Sam said. "I have something to show you."

She waited downstairs while Jackson threw on some jeans and grabbed a coat. He thought about texting his dad in case he came home and found Jackson gone, but then he didn't. It wasn't like his dad really cared where Jackson was.

As he locked the door behind them, Jackson couldn't help but wonder what it would be like to leave his house for the last time—to just leave Grey Hills, and his father, without a word. He suspected it might feel a bit like stepping out of his own body.

The snow hadn't started sticking yet. It came down in huge, wet flakes that managed to cling to Sam's hair and the shoulders of her coat. Jackson thought she looked like one of those angels that you set on top of the Christmas tree, all flocked and electric. He liked how tall she was, and that he didn't really have to look down that much when they spoke.

"How long are you staying?" Jackson asked. They were walking so close that he could have reached over and taken her hand. Their shoulders touched every third step or so.

Sam shrugged. "That really depends on you." As they walked, the snowflakes grew smaller and started to cover the sidewalk. Jackson glanced back and could see their footprints for a few steps behind them. It looked like they had appeared out of nowhere, as if he and Sam were two winged travelers who had just dropped down from the sky.

"Would you go?" he asked, letting his arm bump against hers again. "If you were me, I mean? Would you leave everything? Would you just run away?" A strand of Sam's snow-dusted hair stuck to his jacket. Her red hair looked darker against the white.

Sam swept her hair back out of her face, then wrapped it up into a bun at the back of her neck. Jackson never knew how girls did that—just make their hair stay up without even a hair band. Her ears sort of stuck out when her hair wasn't covering them. Jackson noticed that her ears weren't pierced, and wasn't sure how he could have missed that detail before.

He thought every girl got her ears pierced—it was almost like they were born that way: with a bellybutton and pierced ears. But hers weren't.

They were whole. He added her earlobes to the list of parts of Sam he wanted to examine more closely.

When Sam finally answered him, Jackson had almost forgotten he had asked her a question in the first place. He had been too busy staring at the side of her face, memorizing the way she clenched and unclenched her jaw, and the new shadows that pooled at her neck in the gray light. So when she started talking, Jackson looked down at the snow gathering on the ground. Just in case she might stop talking if he watched her.

"We were fifteen when it happened," Sam began, her voice that flat, faraway tone that people sometimes use when they are telling a story. Especially a story they don't particularly want to tell. "My dad had been working with some people. Trev and I didn't know much about it at the time, but we knew it was top secret, hush-hush kind of stuff. We thought he might have been working with the government, but Dad wasn't supposed to say anything. So, of course, Trev had to start snooping.

He found a file in Dad's office at home. Yeah, I know, right? Who just keeps top secret information lying around their house? But that was our dad. When he was working on something new he never really stopped to think about anything outside of the project.

"Dad was a physicist. Theory, mostly. He was always talking about things you couldn't hold in your hand. Things you could only see in your mind's eye. Particles and waves and relativity. That kind of stuff." She paused, reaching out to shake off the fine layer of snow from a tree branch's naked limb. "Alternate dimensions. That was the big one. He was always talking about the possibility that there were other worlds—whole other galaxies—stacked right on top of each other. 'What if'—those were his favorite words to start any conversation. *What if* you could cut a hole from one dimension to another? *What if* you could walk right through? Well, these men wanted to turn his *what if*s into reality."

"The Doors?" Jackson murmured the question. He really didn't want her to stop talking.

She nodded. "But I don't think he knew that's what they were. I think . . . I think Dad thought those people were actual scientists. That he was making this huge breakthrough. But I think they were just using him. Experimenting on him, maybe? And it made him crazy."

"How did you learn all this?"

"I told you, we found his files. They were just sitting in his file cabinet. It wasn't even locked. And then they contacted us. You know . . . after. We learned more about the agency then. They were not scientists, let me tell you. Not even close."

"Maybe he wanted you to find the files? As a kind of, I don't know, insurance or something? So you'd know?"

She shook her head again. "I don't think he had that kind of clarity, in the end. Before he . . . before it happened, Dad sounded so strange. We would be sitting down to dinner, and he'd say something that made absolutely no sense. Like, one time he asked if our mom had milked the cows yet. We lived in the city. In a fucking apartment. At first I thought he was making some kind of weird joke, but he didn't laugh.

"Another time Trev had his phone out, and Dad stared at it like he had no earthly idea what it was. But other days he'd be just fine—he'd be our Dad again. And he was never violent. He didn't throw things or do anything like that. There was no warning. It was after Trev found the file, and we read about the Doors. We didn't know what they were then, of course, but there was a thumb drive that had the map of the Doors and some other information. It was almost like a ghost-hunting starter kit—all wrapped up with a bow. Just waiting for us.

"That day—that fucking day—it was almost three years ago now. We came home and found them like that, in the kitchen. It looked like Mom had been baking pies for Thanksgiving, and maybe Jamie was helping. He was almost big enough to actually help, you know? He could stand on a stool and mix things with a big spoon without flinging everything all over the floor. Jaime could even crack eggs into a bowl. He was such a good boy, really. He was so much younger than us that it was sometimes hard to even think of him as our brother. I mean, of course he was, but he wasn't a brother the way Trev was . . . Jaime was the baby. He was the one we were all supposed to protect.

"Trev and I found Jamie behind the garbage can, like he had thought he could hide there. He was—" Sam took a deep, gulping breath like she'd forgotten to inhale that whole time she had been talking. She was silent again for a few moments—just breathing in and out like an athlete after a sprint. Or a warrior after a battle.

Jackson took her hand and she let him. He held it loosely, like her hand was a fragile insect—one of those small, blue butterflies perhaps—that he might crush.

"You asked what I would do. Well, that's what I did. When my dad—" she took another deep breath. "When he killed them, I ran. Not that moment. Not right away. But when we could— when we had the money—we ran. And we kept running. That's what I do, Jackson. I run away." For a moment Jackson thought she was crying, but it was just the snow that had melted on her face.

"Trev said it was a ghost . . . that a ghost was inside your father. Possessed him?"

"He wants to believe that."

"But you don't?"

"I don't know. Maybe I do, deep down. But it's so simple, you know? Just blame the ghost. That's why Trev does this. That's why this all started. He convinced himself that it wasn't Dad. That even though it was his hands . . . that he did those things to Mom and to Jamie. That even then, it wasn't his fault. But, you know, even if that was true—even if there was a ghost inside his brain—then he should have fought harder. Dad should have fucking fought for us, you know? Because who else is gonna do it—if even your own dad can't save you? No one will save you, Jackson. You have to save yourself."

Jackson squeezed her hand. "Is that what you do? Save yourself?"

Sam nodded. "And Trev," she said, wiping her nose with the back of her hand. "Someone's gotta look out for him. He's fucking helpless." Sam was smiling again—her small smile that pulled at the corner of her lips. Not her big smile, the one that made her look like herself.

He could just barely see her freckles, and a single snowflake was caught in her eyelashes. She was so beautiful.

Jackson wanted to kiss her then, but it seemed wrong after she had just told him all that. Like he'd be taking advantage of her when her shields were down. Actually, maybe this was what the real Sam looked like after all.

He lifted her hand and laid it against his cheek. Her fingers were cold, but not as cold as the falling snow. And when they reached the big, yellow house, they kept walking right past.

Chapter Nine

Sam held Jackson's hand until they reached the park, the one by the old bunkers. Jackson hadn't said much since Sam told him her story, but that was okay with her. She didn't really want to talk anymore. His hand was warm or at least it was the same temperature as hers. Maybe they were both cold.

The park was empty, and the snow was still falling, but barely. Sam turned her face up to the sky. The snowflakes felt alive, like tiny moth feet touching down on her forehead and cheeks before taking flight again.

"I love the snow," Sam murmured. "I missed it."

"Where did you use to live?" Jackson asked.

"Lots of places. Texas. Wyoming. California for a while. We just keep moving." Sam let go of his hand and walked over to the swing set. Next to the big cement bunkers—those remnants from a past war—the park had a rolling grassy area with a big slide, a swing set, and a merry-go-round.

Sam cleared the dusting of snow off one of the swings and sat down. She didn't really start swinging, but just kind of swayed back and forth, her toes never leaving the ground. Jackson sat in the swing next to her, not bothering to brush away the snow.

They sat in silence for a little while. From her swing, Sam could see out to the water, though it was hard to tell what was water, and what was just more gathering clouds. It was one of Sam's favorite places in Grey Hills, though she hadn't realized it before that moment. On a clear day, when the sun made the water sparkle, Sam felt like she was on the edge of the world.

Sam watched Jackson swing. Well, he didn't really swing either, but let his feet drag in the bark chips that covered the ground beneath the swing set. His legs were so long.

She had been planning to take Jackson back to the yellow house and show him the journal and the freaky blue light in Dom's room. Dominick didn't want Jackson to see it, and Trev was so fucking wishy-washy about the whole thing that Sam wanted to scream. *Whatever you guys think is best,* Trev kept saying, like he couldn't possibly have his own opinion. Sam had decided that Dom could go fuck himself and she was just going to go ahead and show Jackson everything. He deserved that much.

But when they got close to the house, Sam couldn't bear to go inside—not with Dom in there. Sam didn't know if Dom really still thought that Jackson had something to do with Macy's death, or if he just needed to hate someone right now and Jackson was the lucky winner. She couldn't even mention his name without Dom leaving the room. And what if Jackson found out what Dominick had done to Macy's body?

Sam didn't really know what Dom would do if they actually took Jackson with them when they left Grey Hills. But how could they leave Jackson behind? That would be like leaving a really big, gangly puppy out in the snow.

Sam leaned back in the swing. Her hair came loose from the bun, and she could feel the tips of her hair drag on the ground. "Where do you want to go?" she asked, trying to sound nonchalant. Like his answer didn't even matter.

"What do you mean?" Jackson turned to look at her. He had that adorable little half-smile—like his brain didn't quite realize what his mouth was doing.

"When we leave—if you come with us—where would you want to go? We can go anywhere."

"Don't you have a place picked out? Another point on your map?"

Sam shrugged. "Maybe. But maybe that doesn't really matter anymore. Where would you go, if it was up to you?"

"I don't know. I haven't really been anywhere before."

"That's not true . . . you've been here. Grey Hills is somewhere. Just pick another place."

"I guess . . . Alaska? Is that weird? I always liked those shows on the Discovery Channel. You know, the survival ones, where people have to catch fish and eat bugs and stuff. Macy and I . . . " Jackson trailed off.

Sam nudged his leg with the edge of her shoe. "It's okay to talk about her. At least, you can talk to me if you want. What would you and Macy do? I want to know." It was growing colder, and the metal chain of the swing was starting to make Sam's hands go numb. She tried to blame the cold for the way her teeth started to chatter at the mention of Macy's name.

"Well . . . I was just going to say that Macy and

I would sometimes talk about trying out for one of those shows. We weren't serious or anything, at least, I wasn't. I'd probably starve in a day. Macy used to say that I was skinnier than a mosquito's dick." Jackson sort of half-laughed, then stopped talking. He frowned, slightly, and Sam wished she hadn't asked.

She knew that look—what it meant. It was like when you turn over a big rock on the beach, and all of these poor little crabs come scuttling out. That's how Jackson looked—like his heart was trying to crawl out of his chest.

"You're not that skinny, you know. You'd probably last a few days at least," Sam said, trying to smile. "I'd probably end up eating the camera guy after the first day."

Sam looked back out toward the water, then said, "So . . . you and Macy." *Don't ask . . . don't fucking ask him that.* But the words just sort of spilled out of her mouth. "I shouldn't even bring this up, and I'm sorry if it makes me an asshole, but . . . you and Macy? Were you, you know, together? Like . . . I mean, I always figured that you had the *boy-next-door* complex going on. Were you in love with her? Sorry, I just always wondered about that. You don't have to answer if you don't want." She clamped her mouth shut and looked down at the snow gathering on the bark chips.

When Jackson didn't say anything right away, Sam stopped her swing and covered her face with her hands. "Sorry. I *am* an asshole. I can't believe I just said that."

"No. Sam, it's fine. I don't mind." But Jackson didn't look at her while he spoke, so he probably *did* mind. Sam twisted her wet hair around her fingers, wishing she hadn't said anything, but hoping he'd keep talking.

He did. "Nothing happened with me and Macy. I guess . . . well, I suppose, I thought about it sometimes. But I wasn't *pining* away for her or anything. But I did love her. She was my best friend, you know? She was, like, the part of me that I could see. This sounds cheesy, but sometimes it felt like she could read my mind. She was inside my head. One of those little devils or angels that sits on your shoulder and knows all of your secrets. That was Macy. She was the best part of me."

"That's not true." Sam reached over and touched his arm. "You're the best part. You, Jackson. You're a good person," she paused, then whispered, "You're amazing." Sam bit her lip, almost hoping he hadn't heard because it was so fucking cheesy.

Jackson looked down at his hands, but his half-smile was back. "What about you?" he asked, "You and Dom ever, you know?"

"Oh God!" Sam had placed her hands back on the chains and started to drift from side to side rather than back and forth, so every other motion brought her closer to—and then further away from—Jackson. "I suppose I have to answer that now, don't I?"

Jackson nodded emphatically.

"Okay, short answer: Dom and I thought about dating two years ago when Trev and I first sort of adopted him into our group. He was like a little, adorable stray that Trev brought home. Hard to resist, you know? But *thought about* are the key words. We would exchange these really pathetic, charged glanced when Trev wasn't looking, and sometimes Dom would hold my hand if we were watching a movie. But the more we got to know each other, the less I fantasized about kissing Dominick Vega, and the more I wished he would just keep his fucking mouth shut. And that's sort of how it's been ever since. I guess we're friends. But yeah . . . no. Dom and I are *not* and never were a couple."

"Macy thought you two had some kind of a torrid love affair, and you broke his heart."

"No, sorry to disappoint. I think the only one breaking hearts was Macy." Sam put her hand over her mouth. "Fuck, I didn't mean to say that. Sorry Jackson! I don't mean half the things I say."

Jackson stood up and stepped in front of Sam's

swing. He leaned over and grabbed the chains. His face was just inches from Sam's. "You don't need to apologize to me. Ever, Sam."

"Sorry . . . " Sam whispered. There were snowflakes in his lashes and a few melting on his lips. Sam couldn't help but stare at his lips.

Sam pushed the swing forward and kissed him. Then she pulled him down toward her, until he was on his knees, and her hands were on the back of his neck. How long had she been thinking about doing this? At least since that day at the lake, or was it even earlier? Probably, if she was being honest with herself, it was since she saw him the night of the Lock-in, with Lorna's gun pointed at his head.

Something inside her heart had shivered when she saw his face—stricken and hopeless. She had wanted to protect him.

When Sam finally pulled away from the kiss and opened her eyes, she was surprised to see a little girl and her mother walking over to the swings. Sam was sure they had the park to themselves.

Sam stood up. "Come on," she whispered, pulling Jackson with her. Sam didn't want to share this moment with anyone.

They walked past the dark shape of one of the bunkers and ducked behind it. There was a little path that led down to the water, with a steep grassy bank rising up on one side. No one would be able to see them there. The path was slippery, and Sam almost tripped over an exposed root, but Jackson steadied her.

When they reached the gravelly beach she grabbed Jackson's face and pulled him to her. They sank down to the ground. Rocks dug into Sam's back, but she was more aware of Jackson's body along the length of her own. His mouth was warm and tasted like toothpaste.

She ran her hand along his back, but his coat was so thick and completely in the way. He must have been having the same problem because pretty soon he was unzipping her coat. She shivered, but in a good kind of way. Then his hands were under her shirt, and her feet were hooked around his legs. It wasn't enough. She wanted him to be so much closer.

"We can go somewhere else," she murmured. "If you want."

Jackson lifted his head away from her and looked into her eyes. She nodded.

He blushed and smiled that half-smile again. "We could go to my house," he whispered. "My dad should be gone for a while."

She nodded again, then kissed him long and deep, her hands on his jeans. Then she pushed him away. "Okay. Let's go."

As they were standing up, something in the water caught Sam's eye. At first she thought it was just the sun glinting off a small wave, but it was too bright. And blue.

Sam's stomach twisted as she walked closer.

"Sam?" Jackson said, tugging on her hand. She let go of him and bent down over the shallow water. There, just below the surface, was a jagged, blue line of light. It looked just like the one in Dom's bedroom.

Sam gasped and took a few steps back, nearly colliding with Jackson.

"What happened?" he asked, holding her by the shoulders.

Sam pointed to the water. "Can you see it? That light?"

Jackson looked where she was pointed. He squinted and took a step closer. Then shook his head. "I only see water. What do you see?"

"There's a blue light. Right there."

Jackson looked again, then made a small sound and pressed his hand to the side of his head. He closed his eyes tightly, like he was in pain.

"Are you alright?" Sam put her hand on his arm.

Jackson flinched, shrugging her off. "It's nothing," he said.

She took her hand away, then zipped up her coat and crossed her arms. Sam peered over at the blue line again—it looked like a crack in the ground—and took out her phone. She was about to call her brother when she felt something prickly on the back of her neck, like someone was watching her. Sam whirled around and saw the mother and daughter from earlier looking over the side of the bank. They were staring right at her.

Sam hadn't looked closely at them before. If she had, she would have noticed the thin stream of blood trickling out of the woman's nose. And her two black eyes. The child . . . her eyes were completely white, as though they were rolled back entirely into her head. And they weren't staring at her, Sam suddenly realized. There were staring past her. They were watching the blue crack of light as it pulsed beneath the waves.

"Can you see them?" Sam whispered to Jackson. She gestured to the pair.

Jackson furrowed his brow, then frowned. "No," he said. His voice sounded defeated. "I can't see anything."

Chapter Ten

"Now there are cracks?" Jackson asked, looking across the kitchen table to Trev and Dom. "Like, cracks? Not a Door?"

Sam nodded. "Not a Door. It's not . . . I don't know how to explain it. It doesn't feel the same as a Door. A Door is an actual opening to where the dead are. But these . . . I think . . . maybe these are what comes before a Door."

"How do you know that?" Jackson rubbed his head. It was still aching. "Have you seen something like this before? A crack?"

"No," Dom answered, not meeting Jackson's eyes. "Nothing like this."

"Well," Trev spoke up. He was fiddling with his phone. Sam's brother had tried to take a picture of the crack, but it wouldn't show up on the screen. "I mean, there have been smaller Doors. Dom, you've even said the small ones were like cracks, right?"

Dom sighed. "Yeah. I guess I said that. But they still weren't like this. I just . . . I don't know." He glanced at Jackson and then looked down at his hands. Dom was holding a weird-looking book, Jackson noticed.

When Trev and Dom came to check out the blue light on the beach, Jackson had realized that was the first time he had seen Dom since Halloween. And the look he had given Jackson . . . it made his skin crawl. *Dom still thinks I did it*, Jackson had thought. *He thinks I might have killed Macy.* He felt sick to his stomach.

And he wanted to punch Dom in his fucking face.

Sam had given Jackson a kind of helpless look

and then showed the blue light to the guys. Once again, Jackson couldn't really see what they were looking at, but he thought he could feel it. When he had looked into the water where Sam was pointing, Jackson's head seemed to tighten like there was a rope cinching around his skull.

Then they all went back to the yellow house and explained to Jackson that there was also a crack in the ceiling above the kitchen. Or was it in the floor of Dom's room? Whatever. The important part was that there was a blue light that they all said looked like a rip in the fabric of reality (or something that sounded equally freaky).

It was like a Door, but not a Door. A crack.

"And there's more," Sam said.

Dom gave her a sharp look. She shook her head at him and kept talking. "We found something near the crack in Dom's room, under the floorboards. An old journal. We don't really know what to make of it yet."

When Sam said the word *journal* Jackson felt

something twang in the back of his head. It almost felt like déjà vu. "A journal?" he asked.

"Dom?" she said, holding out her hand.

Dom set the book he was holding on the table and slid it to the center. Jackson was about to reach for it, but Sam picked it up. Jackson's empty hands twitched. He pulled them back and clenched them into fists beneath the table.

"See," Sam moved her chair a little closer to Jackson's, "It says *Eli Grey* here. It belonged to one of the Greys."

"Does it talk about the cracks? In the journal, I mean?" Jackson asked. His heart was suddenly racing. He tried to keep his breath steady, but he felt like he couldn't get enough air. "Can I . . . " Jackson paused, wiping his suddenly damp forehead. "Can I see it?"

"Are you okay?" Trev asked, looking up from his phone, his eyebrows raised. "You don't look that good. Are you getting sick? If you're sick do not breathe near me. I don't *do* sick."

Sam rolled her eyes at her brother. "Wow, you're a regular Mother Teresa."

"You're really sweating," Dom added. Then he narrowed his eyes at Jackson. "There's something . . . You look different."

Jackson met Dom's gaze and didn't look away this time. He didn't know how long they stayed like that, with their eyes locked. It was probably just a few seconds, but Jackson felt like Dom wasn't even looking at him anymore. It was like he was looking at something inside his head. And Jackson saw something in Dom that he couldn't fathom. There was a secret in Dom's dark eyes.

Jackson felt himself start to smile, but then he put his hand over his mouth and looked down. He was shaking.

Sam cleared her throat and set the journal back on the table. "Jackson, you really don't look good. Maybe we should talk about this tomorrow?"

"Okay," Jackson said, not looking away from

the small leather book. "But if I could just take a quick look at the journal . . . "

Even as he spoke Dom was reaching across the table to take the journal back. "Have a good night," Dom said to Jackson, dismissing him with a thin smile.

"We'll talk tomorrow," Trev said, looking first at Jackson, and then Dom with a puzzled expression on his face.

Sam offered to walk Jackson home, but he said no. He wanted to be alone.

The sun was already starting to set, and the light dusting of snow cooled his face.

The journal. There was something so familiar about the journal. Jackson opened and closed his empty hands.

They were tingling.

Chapter Eleven

On Sunday morning Dom burst into Sam's room. "The journal's gone!" he whisper-yelled.

"What?" Sam opened her eyes and saw Dom's face peering over her. "Get out of my room!" Then her sleepy brain processed what he had just said. "Gone? What do you mean gone?"

"Gone. Not here. The opposite of *in my fucking hand.*" Dom sat on the edge of her bed, and Sam pulled the covers up around her neck. She liked to sleep naked and they all knew it. "It was on the kitchen table last night, and now it is missing."

"Trev must have it," she said in a groggy

voice. What time was it anyway? Way too fucking early.

"He doesn't have it. He told me to fuck off and
ask you."

"Well, shit. Are you sure it was on the table?"
Sam brushed her hair back out of her eyes, care-
ful to keep her other hand firmly on the blanket.
"And your breath stinks, by the way. Try a tooth-
brush."

Dom wrinkled his nose at her. "You're not exactly a morning rose yourself. Come on, get dressed
and help me look. It didn't just walk away."

But after turning the house upside down for the
next hour, it looked as if that was exactly what the
journal had done. After the first fifteen minutes of
searching, Trev had left to go procure donuts and
"good coffee." So Sam was currently sitting on the
floor in the kitchen, the box of remaining donuts
in her lap, shoving a second maple bar into her
mouth.

"It's not here," Dom said. He was sitting at the

table, just drinking coffee (which Dom had made at home, and which Trev had deemed "crappy," prompting his trip to the store). If Dom didn't start eating more, Sam thought, he was going to move past defined cheekbones to just plain gaunt. And Dom simply didn't have the bone structure to pull it off.

She lifted the box of donuts toward Dom. "Eat," she said.

But Dom just shook his head.

Trev, who was sitting on the floor next to her, took the box. "I didn't buy a dozen donuts so you could eat a dozen donuts," he said. "Save at least one for the rest of us." She stuck her tongue out at him.

Dom cleared his throat. "So, what do we do?"

Sam shook her head, still chewing. Trev shrugged.

Dom rolled his eyes. "We've got the brain trust today, I see. Look, I think it's obvious. Jackson stole the journal."

Sam started coughing on her pastry, then spit it out into her hand. "What?" she said, standing up. She threw the chewed-up piece of maple bar into the sink, and Dom gave her a disgusted look. "Why Jackson?" she said.

"Um, he's the only other person who knew about the journal?" Dom answered. "Could it be more obvious?"

Trev raised his hand. "I hate to be the voice of reason here, but how do we know that no one else knew about the journal? There might be another crazy Lorna out there for all we know. But seriously, I bet we'll still find it somewhere. Why would anyone want to steal the journal anyway? It was a bunch of crazy ramblings."

"It was a clue," Dom said. "It has to have something to do with these cracks. And I think Jackson knows more than he's telling us." He paused, then lowered his voice. "I'm starting to think he might have been working with Lorna all along."

Sam scoffed. "Are you kidding me? Jackson has done nothing but help us. He saved my life, or have you forgotten that small detail?"

"At the lake? As I recall you were only in any danger because he took you out there. Not to mention that you were stupid enough to jump in. I think he's dangerous, and you're just too blind to see it."

"And I think this town is making you crazy," she said. "Which is one more reason why we should just get out of here. Just cut our fucking losses and leave."

Trev sighed. "That's just stupid, Sam. Things are just getting interesting, and you want to leave?"

Dom set down his coffee with a loud thump, spilling brown liquid on the table. "Interesting?" he said. "Are you saying that Macy's death was *interesting*? Or how about that Jackson obviously killed her, and you all are just ignoring it? Is that *interesting*? And I suppose the fact that we showed

Jackson the journal last night, and it's gone today is just an *interesting* coincidence. Jesus fuck! When are you going to take your head out of your ass and see what's going on?"

"I see more than you think I do, Dominick Vega," Trev said, not looking up from the box of donuts. "Just how long were you going to try to keep it a secret?"

Sam's stomach dropped. Trev had found out about Gregory. *Shit.*

Then Trev continued. "At what point did digging up Macy and cutting off her finger became a viable option? You have lost it, Dom. We're all trying to ignore it, but the fact remains that you have lost the fucking plot. And, by the way, it's not going to work. You're not going to bring her back. Since when did you even know how to make a Token?"

"I don't think—" Sam started, but Dom cut her off.

"You know what *I* think?" Dom stood up. He

was shaking. "I think it's about time we call our good friend Gregory and tell him what's going on. What do you think about that, Trev? Or are you still too mad at him for breaking up with you or whatever? Can you just fucking grow up? We need the help."

Trev closed his eyes and leaned his head back against the cabinet. He said in a voice almost too soft to hear, "Don't mention Gregory to me again. Don't ever say his fucking name." Then Trev got up and walked out of the house. He took the box of donuts with him.

"Fuck," Sam murmured. "Dom, why did you do that? You know what it does to him."

"Go ask your boyfriend where the journal is, okay? I'm done with this." Then Dom left too, stomping up the stairs.

Sam looked around the empty room, at the spilled coffee and the half-eaten maple bar that had fallen to the floor. She didn't even remember dropping it. Sam sank back down to the kitchen floor and pulled out her phone. She tried to call Jackson, but there was no answer.

She was about to eat the rest of the maple bar when her phone buzzed. A text from Gregory: *In Oregon. C U soon.*

Sam got up and started packing.

Chapter Twelve

When Claire drove to Jackson's house on Sunday night, she didn't really have a plan. She just sat in her car, waiting. She wasn't sure what she was waiting for . . . she just had a feeling. That *Macy* feeling that sometimes sprang up from the center of her lungs lately. As though Macy was talking to her. *Go see Jackson,* that voice—that feeling—said. *Go talk to Jackson.*

Claire wasn't really superstitious, but she did believe that sometimes the universe spoke directly to you, and you had better fucking listen.

That's how it felt when Claire had first met Macy in junior high—that she was just continuing a conversation that they had started in another lifetime. She never told Macy that because it sounded really sappy and exactly like something Claire's mom might say.

Claire's mom believed in crystals, and marked "bad days" on the calendar when you shouldn't even try to go outside. Her mom was actually really embarrassing, and sometimes Claire wished her mom would go back to her maiden name so people at school didn't know that she was related to the middle-aged hippy who worked in the front office. Her parents had only been divorced for, like, a million years.

That night Claire told her that she was going to see a movie with a friend, a lie that her mom really should have been able to see right through because the only friend Claire ever went to the movies with was Macy. And like Claire would even want to go out and do something fun when her best friend was missing. Jesus Christ. But her mom believed her, and even gave her a twenty and patted her on the head like she was her pet dog instead of her daughter.

It was only about ten p.m. when Claire got to Jackson's, but his house was already dark. Claire realized she didn't actually know what Jackson's dad did for a living. Something at the newspaper, Claire was pretty sure.

For all the hours Claire had spent in Jackson's basement when they were growing up, she hadn't ever been that close to his family. It was sad, of course, when Sally Cooper died. Shocking, more than anything. But it wasn't like Claire actively missed Jackson's mom, not the way Macy had. When they heard that Jackson's mom had cancer, Macy looked like she had been kicked in the stomach.

But when Nick died, that was just . . . no words.

She always kind of thought she and Nick would end up together some day. Not really. Probably not. But that's how the movie of her life would have played out—to put it in *Macy* terms. Macy was always comparing her life to movies, while Claire liked to think of how movies were like *her* life.

Claire had kissed Nick, once, when she was thirteen years old. She had snuck out of Macy's room one night when she was sleeping over and crept down the hall to Nick's bedroom. Claire hadn't really thought about what she was doing at the time, just that she wanted to see what would happen if she was brave enough. In the back of her mind Claire had told herself that she could always pretend she was sleepwalking if Macy caught her.

Claire hadn't knocked on Nick's door, but just went right in. She tiptoed (yes, actually tiptoed—wobbling on the balls of her feet) all the way to Nick's bed. Macy's brother was beautiful. He looked a lot like Macy, with light brown hair, but he had eyes that always looked bigger than you expected. Maybe it was his dark eyelashes (Claire's eyelashes were blond, and she always had to wear mascara if she didn't want to look like a hairless monkey). Or maybe it was just that he raised his eyebrows whenever he looked at Claire, like he was surprised to see her.

When she was close to the bed, Claire could tell that Nick was pretending to sleep. She knew he was awake because his breath was uneven, and he even licked his lips once. Claire leaned over. She put her hand on his forehead, like she was checking his temperature. He opened his eyes, but didn't say anything. He had just turned fifteen, Claire remembered, and that had seemed so old at time. Like Nick wasn't even in the same universe as her, but was an astronaut colonizing a far-off planet. Planet Fifteen . . .

Claire pressed her lips to his, and then turned and ran out the door. That was her first kiss, and she never told anyone, especially not Macy. She and Nick never talked about it. The kiss could have been a dream, but it wasn't. Claire couldn't even remember what the kiss had felt like, it was over so quickly. She mainly remembered that Nick's face had looked like something carved out of the night, and how she had felt his eyes follow her when she left his room.

After Nick died Claire tried not to cry in front of Macy. Nick wasn't *her* brother. He wasn't her . . . anything. But she couldn't help but feel that a part of her future had died with him. A hope, perhaps. A possibility. Not just Nick, but the dream of Nick. And how much more selfish could you fucking get when your best friend just lost her brother?

After half an hour of sitting in her car, trying not to check her phone or fall asleep in the driver's seat, Claire saw the front door to Jackson's house open. Jackson stepped outside. He was just in his boxers and a white T-shirt. No shoes.

He walked onto the front lawn and looked up at the sky. Claire looked up too, and just saw clouds. No stars. No moon. Jackson stood that way for maybe ten minutes, staring up at the sky—illuminated by an orange streetlight. Then he just turned around and went back inside. Fucking weird. Who just stands outside like that, in November? Without even a coat?

She waited another thirty minutes before starting the car and pulling away. When she drove past his house, a shiver went through her whole body. The air almost seemed to crackle, like when you shake out a sheet fresh from the dryer and static electricity sparks across it.

In that moment Claire swore she could taste blood. But it was gone again the next second, as soon as she had completely passed his house. Claire pulled over, hands shaking. She licked her lips, trying to catch that taste on her tongue again.

In the rearview mirror, Claire saw Jackson's door open again. He was dressed this time, with a thick coat and hat. When he started walking down the street, Claire got out of her car and followed him.

What are you doing? Claire asked herself as her breath floated above her in the night air, and she made her footsteps as silent as possible.

Chapter Thirteen

The clouds were starting to clear, and Jackson could see a few stars above him and a small, hazy glimpse of the moon.

Jackson knew he shouldn't have come back here. He even told Sam that he wouldn't—that he would stay away from the woods behind the school. They had to have buried her somewhere out here.

If he could just find Macy's grave . . . but he couldn't really finish that thought. He'd what? He'd cry his helpless tears over her rotting body, just as he had done while she grew cold in his arms? Yes. Definitely. But maybe . . . maybe she still needed his help. Maybe she was still scared and alone and didn't know where she was. What if her ghost didn't know how to find her way home? Something told him to come back here. Some feeling in the pit of his stomach.

Jackson didn't really know how ghosts worked. At least not the way that Sam and the others seemed to. But he couldn't help the feeling that Macy was still out there somewhere. That she wasn't really gone.

He hadn't felt that way when his mom died, but maybe that was just because he hadn't believed in ghosts then. Even now, Jackson didn't think his mom was lingering on earth. His mother hated to be late for anything, and he couldn't imagine her waiting around if there was somewhere else she was supposed to be.

Please. He swallowed back the acid that was building in his throat. *Please let there be a heaven for my mother.* Jackson had never really learned anything about religion growing up, but it felt like a prayer.

The snow wasn't very thick beneath the trees, but the thin layer of white made the whole space feel open and bright. It looked like a light had kindled inside of the snow itself rather than simply being reflected back from the moon. Jackson's feet sank into the snow, through to the decaying leaves beneath. His footsteps sounded loud in his ears—a slightly muffled *shhhh shhhh* every time he picked up his feet.

Jackson didn't even know if he could find the spot where Macy had died. He thought he'd remember exactly where he had held her—the way his arms still remembered her body going still, and the blood . . . so much blood. But as he looked up into the naked, grasping branches of the alder trees, Jackson realized that one tree looked exactly like another. He'd lost it—where the Door had slammed shut. Where Macy's blood had sealed it.

A thick drop of melting snow fell from one of the branches and landed on his shoulder. Snow never stayed around very long in Grey Hills. It usually lasted for a few days, and even then it was only that fresh, splendid white for a single morning before becoming a muddy, slushy mess that was just depressing.

Jackson remembered one year when it snowed two feet—a freak occurrence. He was only about eight or nine years old then, and the snow had covered the cars so they looked like sleeping giants. He had walked to Macy's house, wading through the snow like it was some huge confectionary sea.

When he got to her house, Macy was waiting for him on her front porch. She came running down the front steps and then vanished into the snow. Her feet had slipped out from under her, and then she was lying on her back, almost completely covered by a snow drift.

Jackson had laughed, but then she didn't get up. He trudged over to where Macy had disappeared, and there she was—her wool hat gone, and her light brown hair spread out like she was a frozen mermaid. Macy didn't move. Jackson remembered shaking her shoulder and pulling on her arm, trying to yank her out of the snow. But Macy's eyes wouldn't open, and her arm had just flopped back into the snow when he let go of it.

Jackson had taken a step back and inhaled a single, shuddering breath. *She was dead.* That was the thought that had raced through his brain that day as he stood over her motionless body, which was half-covered with snow. He was about to scream for her parents when Macy sat up and grabbed him around the waist—pulling him into the snow with her.

"Got you!" she had screamed, laughing and laughing until she sucked in some snow and started to cough.

That's what Jackson kept waiting for, he realized. That *Got-you* moment, when it would all be a trick and Macy would really be alive. But he knew that wasn't going to happen. He *knew* she was dead, but he still couldn't *feel* it. Maybe . . . maybe if he could just see her grave. If he could just talk to her again and know that at least a part of her was listening. Maybe then he could start to accept that she was gone. That she wasn't coming back.

"I'm sorry, Mace," Jackson said, trying to make the words sound less fake. Less scripted. "I'm so sorry."

"And just what are you sorry about, Jackson?"

Jackson spun around, wishing he had brought a flashlight. There was a girl, just up the trail where Jackson had come from. "Who's there?"

"What are you sorry about?" she repeated, taking a few steps closer. For an instant Jackson thought—truly thought—that it was Macy's ghost. That she had come back to him. But then Jackson saw how light the color of her hair was in the moonlight.

"What are you doing here, Claire?"

"Following you." Claire stopped when she was about five feet away from Jackson. "Why did you say Macy's name? Why the fuck are you sorry?"

Jackson put his hand over his eyes. His headache

was creeping back—tendrils twisting around the front of his skull. "Let's not do this now. Just . . . let's just both go home, okay?"

"Don't do what?" Even in the darkness Jackson could see that Claire was frowning at him. "Talk about Macy? Where is she, Jackson?"

"Nothing. I didn't mean anything. I just . . . I'm going home."

As Jackson turned away from her, he heard Claire suck in her breath in a quick hiss. "Don't you dare walk away from me Jackson Cooper."

Jackson stopped. His head was pounding. More melting snow fell on his shoulders. "You don't know anything about this Claire." Jackson regretted it the moment he said the words. And he didn't even sound like himself—his voice was ragged. He sounded angry, when all he really felt was a deep, almost numbing sorrow. Why couldn't Claire just leave him alone? Why did she have to keep hounding him like she was Macy's personal avenging angel or some shit?

Claire spoke again. "No, I *don't* know anything, as you put it. I don't know one fucking thing. Where is Macy? Where is she?" He could hear Claire's footsteps behind him—the shuffling of the snow and the snapping of hidden twigs. Then she was right behind him. She was so close that he could practically hear the small frantic flutter of her heart beating in her chest. No, he couldn't possibly hear that, but he somehow felt it—the air vibrating around her. He could almost taste Claire's fear. She was actually afraid of him—imagining all the ways that he could harm her.

Jackson didn't answer. He had nothing to say that wasn't a lie or was too horrible to believe. Jackson wondered, not for the first time, if he should just tell Claire the truth, but Sam had said that he couldn't tell anyone—that bad things would happen. And Sam was right—everyone *would* just assume he did it. That he killed his best friend.

Even Claire thought it. Claire, who had known

Jackson since middle school. Who had spent count-less hours at his house, watching movies and eating the snacks his mom made and the drinks that his parents kept in the fridge. Claire, who knew every-thing about Jackson. Fuck her.

Macy had been afraid of him too. Not when she died, but earlier, before they were friends again. After that long, terrible summer of silence be-tween. Jackson still remembered the way Macy had looked at him when he pulled her into the Chem-istry room. Right before the ghost burned Macy's wrist. Macy actually thought Jackson might do something to her. That he could hurt her. And the worst part was that he had actually wondered if he could.

It wasn't that Jackson wanted to hurt her—he'd never wanted to hurt Macy. But seeing it reflected back in someone's eyes—actually knowing that someone believed the worst of him—made Jackson question himself. What if he was really a bad person? What if underneath his skin there was a second Jackson? A stranger in his own body who could actually do the things Claire was thinking?

From the corner of his eye, Jackson saw Claire slip her hand into her purse. "Where is she, Jackson?" Claire repeated. "You know, don't you? Has she called you?"

"No." Jackson had an almost overwhelming urge to turn and slap Claire. He clenched his hands into fists at his stomach. "I don't know where she is."

"Bullshit. You know. You either know where she is or you did something to her. What did you do? Did you hurt her? Did you hurt Macy?"

Jackson brought his fists up to the sides of his head. "Go away!" The pain was getting worse— shooting down from his head into his neck. He felt sick to his stomach. "Claire . . . I just. I can't do this now. I can't."

Claire put her hand on his shoulder. Maybe it was meant to comfort him, or maybe she just wanted him to turn and face her. Jackson didn't know, and he reacted without thinking. He turned and grabbed her arm, twisting it away from him.

She screamed, and he kept twisting until he thought that the bones in her arm might snap. He wanted to break her arm, he realized with a numb, distant kind of horror. He actually wanted to hear her bones crack.

Jackson's eyes went wide as he met Claire's gaze in the dark. She looked up at him in disbelief. He tried to make himself let go—to tell her that he didn't really want to hurt her, but he couldn't speak. Jackson felt like he was watching himself from far away—like he was a snowdrift melting in the dark.

That feeling—that surge of anger—just kept growing in his chest as the pain in his head grew worse. Thoughts that didn't even sound like his thoughts rang through his pounding head. *Fucking bitch!*

Claire screamed again and raised her free hand. Jackson only had an instant to notice that she was holding something that looked like a dark tube before he heard a hiss and then his eyes were burning.

He let go of her arm and swiped at his eyes. He couldn't open them. His nose was running, and tears were streaming down his face. His face was on fire. He was coughing and coughing, and it wasn't until he was doubled over, spitting into the snow, that Jackson realized Claire had brought pepper spray.

Then something hit Jackson in the face. He fell to his knees in the snow, with his arms over his head. Claire kicked him again, this time in the ribs. "Motherfucker! Never touch me again!" Another kick. "I'll kill you if you hurt Macy! I'll fucking kill you!"

Jackson still couldn't speak because the words he was trying to form were poison. *Bitch!* He wanted to yell. *Stupid whore!* When her boot hit his jaw with a loud crack, sending him reeling into the snow, Jackson's headache abruptly stopped. His whole face was burning from the pepper spray, and her sharp kicks to his jaw and nose. But Jackson's headache was gone.

He lay on his back, arms spread out, and tried to look up at Claire, but his swollen eyes would barely open. "I think I need help," he whispered, tears running down the sides of his face into his already wet hair.

Claire stood over him for a long moment, the cylinder of pepper spray clutched tightly in her right hand. Through his squinting eyes her body looked like a mirage—wavering in and out of existence. "Did you kill her?" Claire finally asked, saying the words quickly, like they would scald her tongue if they stayed in her mouth too long.

Jackson covered his face with his hands. He couldn't speak, but coughed and choked as snot ran down the back of his throat, until he rolled over onto his side and could breathe again. He pressed his face into the snow, though it hardly helped to soothe his burning, itching eyes.

Jackson didn't know how long he lay there,

breathing into the snow, when he heard a man's voice and felt a large, firm hand on his back.

"Dad?" Jackson whispered, but then his arms were wrenched behind his back and something cold and hard circled his wrists. Handcuffs.

Claire had called the police.

Chapter Fourteen

Jackson waited in a room that was empty except for a large table and two chairs. Someone had brought him a paper cup of hot chocolate and an icepack for his face. It was supposed to help his red, swollen eyes and his jaw that was still throbbing from Claire's kick. Her boots had sharp fucking toes.

There was also a big clock on the wall, and it made a loud *tick-tick* with each passing second. He couldn't focus on the clock, and the time just ticked forward until the sound of the clock blended in with his own heartbeat and became meaningless. Jackson didn't know what, or who, he was waiting for, but at least he didn't have to wear the handcuffs while he sat there.

His mouth was dry, so even though the sweet smell of the hot chocolate sort of turned his stomach, he took a small sip. It had gone cold and left a chalky residue on his tongue. He took another sip, then pushed the cup away.

There was a large mirror on the left wall of the empty room, and Jackson wondered if it was one of those two-way mirrors that you always saw in cop shows. Was someone watching him right now?

Jackson stood up and walked over to the mirror. His eyes still hurt, even after someone at the police station had flushed them out with water. He had to fight the urge to squeeze them shut when he looked in the mirror. Jackson thought that he might be able to see a difference in the glass if he looked really closely—that he would be able to tell if there were people on the other side looking back at him.

All he saw was his own haggard reflection.

His eyes were rimmed in red, and he could see the little veins in the whites of the eyes. A sickly yellow bruise was starting to spread along his jaw. Jackson had never thought he was the best-looking guy to start with, what with his big gawky nose, but he looked disgusting now. He sat back down.

He was about to take another sip of the cold hot chocolate, when someone said his name.

"Jackson?" It was a girl's voice, but so soft that at first he thought he had imagined it in the silence. But then he heard it a second time, slightly louder. "Jackson."

"What?" he whispered back, covering his mouth with his hands and glancing at the mirror. He didn't want whoever was on the other side to think he was talking to himself—just in case there *was* another side.

"You look terrible." The voice sounded like it came from right behind him, but when he whipped his head around, the room was still empty.

"Macy?" he whispered, his own voice barely

more than an exhale into his shaking hands. Who-ever was talking to him didn't sound quite like Macy . . . but it didn't exactly sound *unlike* her. It didn't actually sound like a real voice at all, but more like how your voice sounds inside your head. Silent, but everywhere at the same time.

"What happened to you?" the voice asked.

Jackson tried to laugh, because it was funny when he stopped to think about it. Funny how fucking pathetic he had become. "Claire kicked me in the face and called the cops on me."

Was he actually talking to himself? Did he have some sort of brain damage? Speaking of damage, when had Claire learned to kick like that? Was she a secret black belt or something? A tiny blonde ninja?

The voice didn't answer him again for almost a full minute—long enough that Jackson was pretty sure he had just invented the whole thing. He was about to take another sip of the nasty chocolate crap when he heard, "You probably deserved it."

"Yeah," Jackson whispered into his cup. "Yes. I think I did."

"Get your shit together, Jackson. Get a grip, okay?"

"Macy?" he whispered again, his hand holding the cup shaking. The hot chocolate sloshed so violently that he had to set the cup back down. He waited and waited, but he didn't hear anything else. Nothing, that is, besides that insistent *tick-tick-tick* of the clock.

He imagined throwing the paper cup at the mirror—how satisfying it would be to watch the chocolate splash across the perfectly smooth surface. But he didn't touch the cup again. After all, he didn't want the cops to think he was violent or crazy. Because he wasn't crazy . . .

Jackson heard a sound like ice cracking. A thin, glowing line formed in the very center of the mirror, right where he had been staring too intently and spread out in all directions like a spider's shimmering web. All at once a hundred pieces of glass dropped to the floor.

Pushing back his chair, Jackson spilled the cup of hot chocolate across the table. He stepped across the shards of mirror and pressed his hand to the blank wall where the mirror used to be. Not a two-way mirror after all. For some strange reason it was a relief to know.

Jackson picked up one of the pieces of mirror. For a moment he was convinced that the edges were glowing a pale, watery white, or maybe a really light blue. He turned it over and over in his hand, unsure if he was seeing a perfectly normal piece of broken glass, or if it was something more. Had he somehow broken the mirror just by thinking about it? What was that called? Not telepathy . . . Telekinesis, that was it. But that wasn't possible, right?

Fuck if Jackson knew what was *possible* anymore.

Just before the door opened and two policeman with guns came in the room and told Jackson to drop the glass and put his hands where they could see them, he thought he saw something move in the broken shard of mirror. Not something . . .

someone. A man with dark hair, standing just behind Jackson's shoulder, looking into the mirror with him.

Jackson blinked, and the man in the broken mirror vanished. Then he opened his hands and let go of the glass. As Jackson raised his hands a thought crossed his mind. *I could kill them all if I wanted.*

His now-familiar headache began to pound again, and he had to stop himself from smiling.

Chapter Fifteen

It was a little past midnight and there was no way Claire was going to be able to sleep. Not in a million years. After she called the police and told them where to find Jackson, Claire had gone straight home. Her mom asked her how the movie was, and Claire managed to say, "Fine," and escape to her room without further interrogation, but all she could think was, *What have I done?* and *What's going to happen now?*

Claire sat cross-legged on her bed and checked her phone. No missed calls. No emails. No texts. No Facebook messages. Nothing from Macy. Not one fucking thing. Claire wanted to throw her phone against the wall and watch it break into a thousand tiny, jagged pieces of plastic. But she didn't. She wasn't crazy . . .

Macy had been missing for six days. Six days of Claire waiting for her phone to ring—waiting to hear Macy's voice.

"Macy is dead," Claire whispered, still looking down at her silent phone.

Claire had started to make herself say those words out loud at least once a day. *Macy is dead.* At first Claire told herself that she needed to face the worst possibility—that if Macy was dead, it would make it easier if she started to process it now. But in reality those words meant the exact opposite.

Saying, "Macy is dead," actually meant that Macy was still alive because Claire wasn't trying to pretend otherwise. It was like a deal with the universe: if she said the worst possible thing, then it wouldn't turn out to be true. Claire knew it didn't make sense, but it didn't have to. There was no one else in the fucking room. She could talk to herself all she liked.

Tonight, Claire added, "Jackson killed Macy." Those words were even harder to say.

Her arm still hurt where Jackson had grabbed her in the woods a few hours ago. At the time, Claire seriously thought that he was going to break her arm. Stupid fucker. Stupid, goddamn mother-fucker.

Just thinking about Jackson made her so furious that she wanted to break something. Not her phone anymore—she needed her phone—but she grabbed a little ceramic horse off her desk and threw it against the wall. It just bounced off, and fell to the baby-blue carpet perfectly in-tact. Piece-of-shit horse couldn't even break properly.

Claire thought about walking over and stomp-ing on the horse's head but her heart wasn't in it anymore, and she was even starting to feel sorry for the little figurine. Her dad had given it to her when she was nine, and she had named it Moonbeam because a friend at her old school had an actual horse named Moonbeam and Claire wasn't very good at coming up with original names.

She checked her phone again.

She checked her phone.

She picked up her phone and called Trev.

"Hello?" Trev always answered slowly and kind of skeptically—as if he had no idea who was calling. Or perhaps like he knew who it was, but he thought they might have called him by mistake.

Claire sighed, loudly. "Are you awake?"

"Pretty sure I'm sleep-talking. You?"

She walked over and scooped Moonbeam off the carpet. "Can I come over?" Now that she had a closer look, Claire saw that there was a chip in the horse's ear. Claire set the horse back on her desk and pressed her finger and thumb to the bridge of her nose.

Trev didn't answer right away, and Claire thought she could hear someone talking in the background. It sounded like a girl's voice, which meant that it was probably Sam. Not Macy. It couldn't be Macy.

Unless . . .

Claire didn't wait for Trev's reply. "I'm just gonna come over. I already have my keys in my hand. Be there in five minutes." Claire hung up and took a deep breath. It seriously couldn't be Macy. Stop thinking it might be Macy.

"Macy is dead," Claire said again, her words barely louder than an exhaled breath.

She had to walk past her sister's door on her way to the stairs. Pausing, Claire listened to the silence. Sabrina, or Beenie as Claire called her, was twelve years old and she always slept like the dead. When they used to share a room in their old house, Claire would sometimes watch her sister in her bed across the room and stare at her back until she was sure it was rising and falling.

When Nick died, Claire had tried to imagine losing Beenie, but she couldn't. Her brain couldn't even attempt the fictional scenario. It was literally unthinkable. That's how it felt, now, when she tried to tell herself that Macy was dead. Her brain told her to fuck off.

Actually, almost fifteen minutes passed from the time Claire hung up the phone and when she arrived at Trev's house. She hoped he was still awake and hadn't passed out in the time since she had spoken to him. Claire was not in the mood for whatever personal demons made Trev get sloppy drunk every other day and then need an extended heart-to-heart with the toilet.

Claire didn't ring the doorbell, but just tried the knob. The door swung open. She hoped Trev had unlocked it for her, and that they didn't just leave their front door wide open for any sicko or throat-slasher who happened to walk by. She locked it behind her and went into the kitchen where she found Trev and Sam waiting for her.

Not Macy. She hadn't really thought that it would be Macy.

"Hey," Claire said, tossing her purse onto the table. "Did you know that Jackson's in jail?"

"What?" Sam stood up, her hands running over her long braid. "Jail?"

Claire pulled out a chair, but didn't sit. She gripped the back of the chair so hard that her knuckles turned white. "He attacked me." She paused, and licked her lips. "I think he hurt Macy."

Sam shook her head. "Not Jackson." Sam brought the end of her braid up to her lips, then threw it back over her shoulder. She walked around the table until she was looking down at Claire. "Wait, did you call the cops on him? On Jackson?"

"He. Attacked. Me." Claire took off her coat, rolled up her shirt sleeve, and showed Sam the newly formed bruises on her arm. "He tried to break my arm. I swear to god."

"No." Sam shook her head. "That doesn't make sense."

Claire let her sleeve fall back down. "You know that he attacked Macy, too, right? Last summer? Did he tell you that? That he kissed her and practically mauled her before she pushed him off?"

Sam didn't speak for a long moment. Then she said, "Get out of my house." Her voice sounded like razor wire.

Claire didn't let herself flinch. "Seriously? Don't be stupid, Sam. Jackson may be your boyfriend or whatever, but protecting him? When he might have done something to Macy? Really?" Claire glanced toward Trev, but he just looked down at his hands, which were still wrapped around his phone.

Sam closed her eyes and took a deep breath.

Claire thought Sam might be about to cry, but when she opened her eyes again, her face was an empty mask. It was pretty fucking terrifying. Claire moved toward her purse, where she still had her pepper spray.

"Claire?" Sam said through gritted teeth. "This is what you're going to do. You're going to call the police and tell them that you made it all up. Jackson didn't touch you. You made a big mistake. You're going to do that right now."

"You're really helping him?" Claire picked up her purse off the table and settled it back on her shoulder. "Is this some kind of a game to you? If you did something to Macy, I swear to God. I swear . . . " Claire settled her purse back onto her shoulder—ready to reach in and call 911, or grab her pepper spray. She was starting to wish that she had a gun.

Then Trev stood up. "This isn't . . . this is just a misunderstanding."

"No," Claire interrupted him. "I don't think

it is. I think your sister is threatening me. Is that right, Sam? Are you fucking threatening me?"

Then Sam smiled. If Claire thought Sam's "blank" face was unnerving, she was not prepared for her smile. The tall girl looked like something feral—a werewolf caught between transformation. A person and a beast sharing the same face.

"Claire?" Sam said through gritted teeth. "Do you have any idea what I could do to you? In this house? Right now? And this isn't a threat. This is a fucking lesson in basic manners. You come into my house and start throwing around your theories like some kind of sparkly Veronica Mars? How long have you known Jackson? Where is your loyalty? You throw him under the bus the moment he doesn't *smile* enough for you? News flash, his best friend is missing. He is *fucking depressed.* And now you've called the cops on him? Get the fuck out of my house!"

Claire made herself smile back and was just trying to think of what she could possibly say when, out of the corner of her eye, she saw Dom walking into the room.

"Sam, we have to tell her." Dom's voice was gravelly, like he had a bad cold. Or . . . like he'd been crying.

When he stepped into the better light of the kitchen, Claire took in his bare feet and his faded jeans. She looked at his rumpled blue sweatshirt, and then, finally, when there was nowhere else to look, she made herself look at his face.

Claire hadn't realized how long it had been since she'd actually seen Dominick. He must have been skipping class. Had she even really seen Dom since Macy went missing? Maybe not, because she would have known just from looking at his face. She would have seen it in the hollows of his eyes, in the defeated lines of his face.

Dom didn't look like someone who had stayed up all night worrying. He didn't look like someone who was waiting for the phone to ring. He looked like someone who already knew how the story ended, and it had shattered him.

"Macy's dead," Claire whispered. There was nothing else to say.

Chapter Sixteen

Jackson's dad picked him up from the police station a little after one a.m. The police had woken his dad up, and Frank Cooper looked like it, with his hair sticking up in the back, and there was a line from the pillow on his cheek. His dad never yelled when he was angry, he just got quiet.

Apparently Claire wasn't going to press charges. That's what his dad told him on the nearly silent drive from the police station back to their house.

"What were you doing out there?" his dad asked, not taking his eyes off the road. "And what did you do to Claire? You hurt her. That's what they said on the phone. They said that she got you with pepper spray?" Jackson had never heard his dad's voice sound so cautious before, like he was trying to dismantle a bomb with his words. Cut the blue wire.

"Nothing. I was just out. I needed some air."

"Just out? That's bullshit, son. You don't just go out walking in the middle of the night unless you're in some fucking Patsy Cline song." Jackson flinched. The last time he heard his dad swear was right after they got his mom's cancer diagnosis, and Frank Cooper punched a hole in the wall.

His dad almost broke his hand, and Jackson's mom had told his dad that he wasn't allowed to melt down because he had to be there for Jackson after she was dead. Jackson had been in his bedroom at the time and probably wasn't supposed to hear them, but the walls were so thin.

"Claire and I were looking for Macy." Jackson was getting used to speaking in half-truths. He wasn't going to tell his dad that he had actually been looking for Macy's body. Or her ghost.

His dad turned into their driveway. "You were looking for her in the woods? In the middle of the night? And why, exactly, did Claire beat the shit out of you and call the police?"

"It was a misunderstanding. She just got worked up. You know how she is." Jackson wasn't actually sure what Claire *was* anymore except seriously pissed off at him. And a pain in his ass. He wondered why Claire had dropped the charges. Maybe because *she* had beat the shit out of *him,* as his dad put it. Maybe because Jackson hadn't really hurt her.

He remembered how fragile Claire's arm had felt in his hands. How easy it would have been to just snap her bones. How he had wanted her arm to break . . .

Jackson didn't wait for his dad to turn off the car before unbuckling and opening the passenger door. He hopped out and started walking toward the house.

"Wait a minute," his dad called as he slowly

got out of the car. "What about the mirror at the station? You're paying me back for that." Jackson didn't know when his dad had started to move like an old man. He wasn't even that old—not even fifty yet—but he took slow, measured steps as he walked toward the front door. It looked like there was too much gravity, or maybe as though there was some other unseen force pushing down on his shoulders.

Did I do this to him? Jackson wondered. *Or is it still Mom?*

"I didn't break that mirror," Jackson finally answered while he waited for his dad to unlock the front door. Jackson couldn't explain what had happened at the station, or the voices he was hearing. Had he really seen that man in the broken piece of mirror? What did that mean? He needed to talk to Sam.

After they both walked in the house, his father gave Jackson a long look—like he was trying to find something in Jackson's face. Finally, he said,

"I'm going to bed. We'll discuss this in the morning. With Claire's mom and dad."

"Her dad doesn't live here," Jackson muttered.

His dad wiped a palm across his forehead. "Her mom then. We need to talk about this. Maybe you should see a counselor. Jesus, first your mom, then Macy's brother. I should have done something earlier. This is my fault."

And Macy. Jackson silently added his best friend to his dad's morbid list.

"Okay," Jackson said. "Yeah, I can go see someone. That's fine. That'll help." *Nothing will ever help,* he didn't say. *Nothing can fix this.*

I can help, a voice whispered in his head. A man's voice that sounded almost like Jackson's own thoughts, but not quite. Older, perhaps. Deeper.

As Jackson walked up the stairs toward his bedroom, he wondered why he wasn't more concerned that he was hearing voices. He wondered why he wasn't picking up his phone to call Sam RIGHT NOW. But when he thought about taking his phone out of his pocket a sleepy sort of calm trick-led down the back of his mind. He just wanted to sleep.

To sleep, perchance to dream, he thought briefly. But he didn't know why he thought that either. He hated Shakespeare.

When Jackson got to his room his eyes were already closed, and his breathing was deep and even. He locked the door behind him and then knelt beside his bed. Jackson then pulled the journal out from beneath his mattress. Opening it to the middle of the book, Jackson pressed the pages to his cheek. "Almost ready," he whispered to himself. "Almost time."

Chapter Seventeen

Claire didn't go home after she left Trev and the others. At the time, she had hardly believed that—after all the things they had told her—they were just going to let her leave. But when Claire had stood up and said she needed to go home before her mom missed her, they didn't try to stop her.

She drove around the block once and then came back and parked her car just down the street from the yellow house. It wasn't actually yellow at night. It had no color. It could have been any house, in any place. Anyone could have lived there. But Sam, Dominick, and Trev weren't just anyone, were they? Not if the things they had told her were true.

Ghosts. What the fuck was Claire supposed to do with *ghosts*? Claire could almost feel their words still fluttering around her head like tiny, insistent birds. Ghosts. Claire was not only supposed to accept that Macy was dead, but she was supposed to believe that a ghost had killed her.

Claire figured she had two options. One, she could call the police right now and watch while the blue-and-red flashing lights surrounded the house. That was the only option that made any sense. That was what smart people did—call the cops and let them decide if the people who had just told you that your best friend was murdered by a ghost were insane or not.

Actually, Claire couldn't quite believe that she wasn't picking up her phone at that very moment and dialing 911. Claire had a feeling, though, a sensation in the center of her chest that had started to feel like a second heart beating. There was something telling her to wait. And not just to wait, but to watch. To keep her eyes on that house.

Her mom always said that you had to trust that little voice in your head—your gut instinct—for really important decisions. Of course, Claire's mom thought that your *gut* had something to do with reincarnation, and that it was your past life speaking to you, so who knew how helpful that advice really was.

Ghosts, though. Was Claire really expected to believe in ghosts now? Had Macy believed in ghosts?

For all Claire knew they had murdered Macy themselves in some fucked-up occult ritual and they were going to kill her next. She had heard of things like that before.

There was that article about two teenage girls who tried to sacrifice a little kid to some forest god they had invented. Claire thought the child had lived, but she couldn't quite remember. But the point was that those two girls had really and truly believed that they were doing the right thing. They thought it made sense to stab a child ten times and leave her bleeding in the woods. What if Trev and the others were just as crazy?

Fuck. What should I do? What would Macy do?

As Claire sat in the driver's seat of her car, thinking out each of her options to every possible conclusion, her eyes started to get heavier and heavier. She closed her eyes and pictured sitting in a courtroom, pointing her finger dramatically at Sam and the others. Then she tried to imagine that ghosts really did exist.

Were ghosts just wandering the street and she couldn't see them? Had Claire ever accidently walked through a ghost? The image of Nick's ghost just floating around like some sort of untethered balloon popped into her head. What if Nick's ghost was watching her right now? What if he had seen her take a shower or go the bathroom?

What if Macy could come back?

At some point Claire fell asleep, which was so stupid that when she jolted awake she was immediately covered in cold panic sweat. She didn't know how long she had been asleep, but it was still dark outside the car window.

Claire looked at her phone. She had a text from Trev, a few hours old now: *U OK?* Yeah, sure. As if *okay* could ever be applied to this situation. Claire did not text back.

Then she heard it—the sound that must have woken her up in the first place.

Sirens.

Chapter Eighteen

Jackson woke up in a graveyard. His phone was ringing. He blinked and tried to rub his eyes but there was a shovel in his hand. *What the fuck?*

He looked around wildly. Rows of worn, crumbling gravestones surrounded him. Jackson's breath caught in his throat. *What am I doing here?*

His phone kept ringing. Jackson dropped the shovel and dug the phone out of his pocket. His hands were covered in mud.

"Hello?" he said in a shaky voice. Huge, wispy clouds raced across the still-dim sky. *What time was it?*

"Jackson?" It was Sam.

"Yeah?" Jackson was so tired it felt like shards of glass were stuck in the corners of his eyes. His teeth were chattering, and he realized he wasn't wearing a coat. How did he get here?

"I'm outside your house. In Dom's car. We're leaving now." Sam spoke so fast that he almost couldn't understand her.

"What?"

"I'm outside your house. We have to go. They found Macy's body. I think they're coming for you." Jackson could hear sirens. He glanced around in the darkness for the blue-and-red lights. There was only darkness. Then he realized that he was hearing the sirens over the phone.

"The cops are there now?" he asked.

"Just come downstairs. We have to go. Don't even grab anything, just run."

Jackson looked up at the sky again. His head hurt. He could hear his blood pounding in his ears. "I'm not at home."

"Okay, good. Where are you? I'll come get you."

Jackson almost said *in a graveyard*, but he heard himself say, "I'll meet you at your house."

I didn't say that, he thought. *That wasn't me.*

"Just tell me where you are. I'll pick you up."

"No. I'm on my way there." Then Jackson hung up the phone. He was so cold, but it didn't matter. He had something he needed to do.

What? Jackson stopped himself. *What am I doing?*

Then Jackson's head hurt so badly that his vision flickered and he bent over. All of the headaches before felt like nothing compared to the pressure threatening to split his skull in half. Even though it was cold, his face was sweating. He knew there was something he needed to do, but Jackson also realized it wasn't his thought. All the sleepwalking and the lost time. Something was wrong. Something was terribly wrong.

Jackson pulled his phone out of his pocket to call Sam, but his hand started to shake and he dropped the phone into the snow.

"No!" Jackson cried out. "Stop it." He felt hollowed out like a pumpkin, but instead of a candle, a fucking bonfire was alight inside his chest. *I need to tell Sam,* Jackson thought again, but that thought was just a whisper beside the gusting scream that was echoing in his head. A man's scream.

Somewhere, in the back of his mind a door opened. He remembered the ghost in the movie theater, the woman who had called him Eli. Jackson remembered the image of the man in the broken glass of the police station. And then more memories. Memories that weren't his. He remembered a knife and a book. He remembered Mabel smiling. He remembered an explosion, and the way his body had lifted off the ground. An explosion that was as bright as the closing Door.

Jackson remembered the hand reaching out from the Door—reaching into his brain.

He sank to his knees, holding his head and trembling. Something was breaking inside him. Jackson felt something wet running down onto his upper lip. He tasted blood. Jackson tried to stand up, but a wave of nausea washed over him, and he threw up onto the ground.

Stop fighting, a soft voice said. A girl's voice. *Stop fighting him. He'll kill you if you fight him.*

"What?" Jackson whispered. He held his hands out in front of his face. They were glowing, just as they had in the theater. Another wave of nausea broke across him.

Let go, Jackson, The girl's voice said again.

So Jackson stopped and let go of his body the same way a swimmer would stop fighting a rip tide. The headache stopped almost immediately. He felt his lips form a smile.

"That's better, isn't it?" Eli Grey said with Jackson's voice. Without the blinding headache, the door in Jackson's mind opened wider, and he realized that he could hear Eli's thoughts. He knew exactly what Eli was planning, because, in that moment he *was* Eli.

Eli stopped and stretched his hands out in front

of him, watching the light that glowed in his hands spread up his arms. This body was young like the last one, but taller. Eli couldn't remember being alive and seventeen, but now here he was.

He could feel this boy's heart pumping in his chest. It was familiar—the blood that sang to him. The bones that carried him. It all felt so . . . right. And now that the boy had finally stopped fighting him, Eli could feel the real potential in this body. He was strong, for a child. And so tall. These legs would take him where he needed to go.

And where he needed to go was the yellow house on the edge of the water. He still had work to do, before the new Doors would open.

Chapter Nineteen

Sam had been waiting for Jackson for about twenty minutes when she heard a knock at the door.

"Where the fuck were you?" she started to say as she opened the door, then the words caught in her throat. It was Gregory.

Shit. She had completely forgotten about Gregory.

"Nice to see you too," Gregory said. His hair was longer than she remembered, and it fell into his eyes. He was wearing a raincoat that looked new and faded jeans. "Can I come in?"

"You're here early," Sam said, not stepping

aside. She tried to picture where Trev was at that moment and if there was any way to prevent what was about to happen. *Shitty shit.*

"Sorry. Thought I'd catch you guys before you skipped town," he said it in a joking tone of voice, but Sam knew he was looking past her, to the suitcase that was still sitting by the stairs. "You were, weren't you?" He looked a bit like she'd just slapped him.

"Gregory, this isn't a good time."

Sam was still trying to think of a way to get Gregory out of the house when she heard Trev behind her. "Where the fuck is Jackson? We're leaving in five, with or without him."

Sam turned in time to see the look of absolute shock on her brother's face.

"Gregory's here." Sam said, her voice going a little high pitched.

"I can see that," Trev crossed his arms.

"Trevor," Gregory said, stepping past Sam into

the entryway. "It's been a while." His face was tense, like he was bracing himself for a fight.

"And how exactly did you find us?" Trev asked.

Sam closed the front door and stepped between them. "I called him." When Trev didn't speak, she said, "We need help, Trev. This is all . . . it's too much."

"You called him?" Trev repeated, not taking his eyes off Gregory. "You fucking *called* him?"

"Trev," Gregory started to say, but Trev cut him off.

"How dare you come here. How dare you . . ."

Dom must have heard voices because he came downstairs. "Oh shit! Hey Gregory."

"Hey Dominick. How's it going?"

"No," Trev said, his voice growing loud. "No *How's-it-going?*. You need to leave. Now."

"I'm here to help you," Gregory said. Sam could see the hurt in his eyes. "I've only ever wanted to help."

"I don't care," said Trev. Then her brother left

the room and walked out the sliding glass door in the kitchen that led to the backyard.

Gregory looked to Sam and then sighed. He followed Trev outside.

Sam met Dom's eyes. He shook his head, as confused as she was. Trev had never actually told them why he and Gregory had broken up, or why he hated him so much. Sam was trying to think of something to say to fill the awkward silence when she heard the door open behind her.

"Jackson!" she cried, about to throw her arms around him when he struck her across the face. She fell to the ground, holding her hand to her throbbing eye.

"What—?" Dom started, but then he was knocked off his feet by an unseen force. Dom's body flew backwards, and his head hit the wall with a loud crack.

Sam looked up with her one good eye and saw Jackson's arms raised in front of him. They were glowing. Then he turned to her. He was smiling.

"You're going to help me," Jackson said. "We're going to have such fun."

Then he grabbed Sam by the neck and started dragging her upstairs. That's when she felt it: a darkness, thick and oozing like molasses. The realization hit her like a knife to the stomach. *There was something inside Jackson.*

She tried to speak, but his hand was so tight that she couldn't even breathe. Sam held onto his arm as her feet thumped along each step. He was so strong.

Once they were up the stairs Jackson walked her to Dom's room, opened the door, and pushed her inside.

She fell to the ground, gasping for breath. She made herself stand up, leaning against Dom's bedframe. "Fuck you," Sam spat at him, though her voice was barely more than a throaty whisper.

Jackson smiled, and then backhanded her again. Sam's lip split open. She got back up and threw herself at him, her arms circling his waist. She managed to knock him against Dom's desk, and the laptop fell off with a loud crash.

Then she heard a crackling sound, and it felt like she was hit by a wall. Sam flew backwards, hitting the bed and rolling onto the ground. Her whole body hurt. She looked up at Jackson, and his arms were glowing again.

"You're strong," Jackson said, smiling. "I think you'll be perfect." There was a bruise blooming on his cheek from where his head had hit the desk. He was covered in mud, she suddenly noticed, and there was blood on his face. Blood that had already dried.

Sam tried to get up again, but her arms wouldn't work right. The room was starting to spin. She watched as Jackson lifted off the floorboard that covered the blue light of the crack. Then he grabbed Sam by her hair and dragged her across the floor until her face was inches from the light.

"Do you hear them?" Jackson whispered into

her ear. "Do you hear them crying out? They want to be free. You're going to help me."

At first Sam couldn't hear anything except the blood rushing in her ears and Jackson's breathing. "Jackson?" she pleaded. "Jackson, what happened to you?"

She closed her eyes against the undulating blue light, but she could still see it against her eyelids. And she could feel it—the power reaching up to meet her. It wasn't pain she felt as the crack began to consume her. It felt like a tingling numbness that began in her brain and seeped down to the tips of her toes. Whatever was inside her—her soul, or whatever it was that made her *Sam*—was draining out into the light in the floor. And the light was growing brighter and deeper.

"I'm not Jackson," Sam heard him say, as though from a great distance. "My name is Eli."

She struggled against Jackson again, but his hands were like a rock formation. Timeless and immovable. It was like drowning, Sam realized.

When she was in the lake, all she could think of was how stupid it was that there was so much oxygen right above her head, but she couldn't reach it. How poorly their bodies had been designed. So much oxygen everywhere, but her body couldn't use it.

This time, her life was the air. The blue light was breathing her in.

Then she heard them. So many voices. Hundreds. Thousands. Too many to count. There weren't words, just pain and anger. Sorrow. It was too much.

It filled Sam's head until it was all she could think. All she could see or hear. She was going to drown in the voices.

Then she felt herself being ripped away from the voices. She opened her eyes and saw the ceiling. Sam lay on her back and sucked in deep breathes until her lungs felt like they might burst. She sat up and scooted back against a wall.

There was Jackson, standing with his back

against the window. Gregory and Trev were in the doorway.

"Who are you?" Jackson asked, staring at Gregory. He didn't sound upset or disappointed. Whatever was inside Jackson was smiling, like he was about to unwrap a big fucking present.

Gregory didn't answer, but reached out a hand and twisted. Jackson fell to his knees, clutching his chest. Sam watched as Jackson writhed on the ground, kicking his feet and knocking his head from side to side. Blood started to trickle from the corner of his mouth.

"Stop it," Sam whispered. Her voice wouldn't work. "Stop," she said a little louder. She wobbled to her feet, pressing her hands against the wall to steady herself.

Jackson was curled into a ball and was letting out a soft keening sound. Blood was seeping from his ears and nose. Gregory was killing him.

"Stop," Sam said again, then lurched toward Jackson. She flung her body across his, though she knew that wouldn't actually help. Not against Gregory. She put Jackson's head across her legs and held him while blood ran down his face like tears.

"Sam?" Jackson asked, rolling his eyes up toward her. "It hurts." Then he went limp in her arms.